Korean Folktales
Four Feminist Retellings

KOREAN FOLKTALES

four feminist retellings

Alpha Sisters Publishing, LLC
5174 McGinnis Ferry Road #348
Alpharetta, GA 30005
alphasisterspublishing.com

Original Korean Edition, 페미니즘으로 다시 쓰는 옛이야기, published in 2020 by IFBOOKS Korea

English Edition, Korean Folktales: Four Feminist Retellings, published in 2023 by Alpha Sisters Publishing, arranged via Bestun Korea Agency

Written by Ziihiion, Sunyoung Cho-Park, Joyce Park, Youngmi Baek-Youn, Sookyeol Ryu
Translator: Kayoung Kim, Peace Pyunghwa Lee
Editor: E. Ce Miller
Publisher: Seo Choi
Book Designer: Sheenah Freitas
Illustrator: Ji In Im

Library of Congress Cataloging-in-Publication Data is available upon request.

First Edition
ISBN 978-1-7334756-8-6 (Paperback)
ISBN 978-1-7334756-9-3 (e-book)

Printed in the United States of America

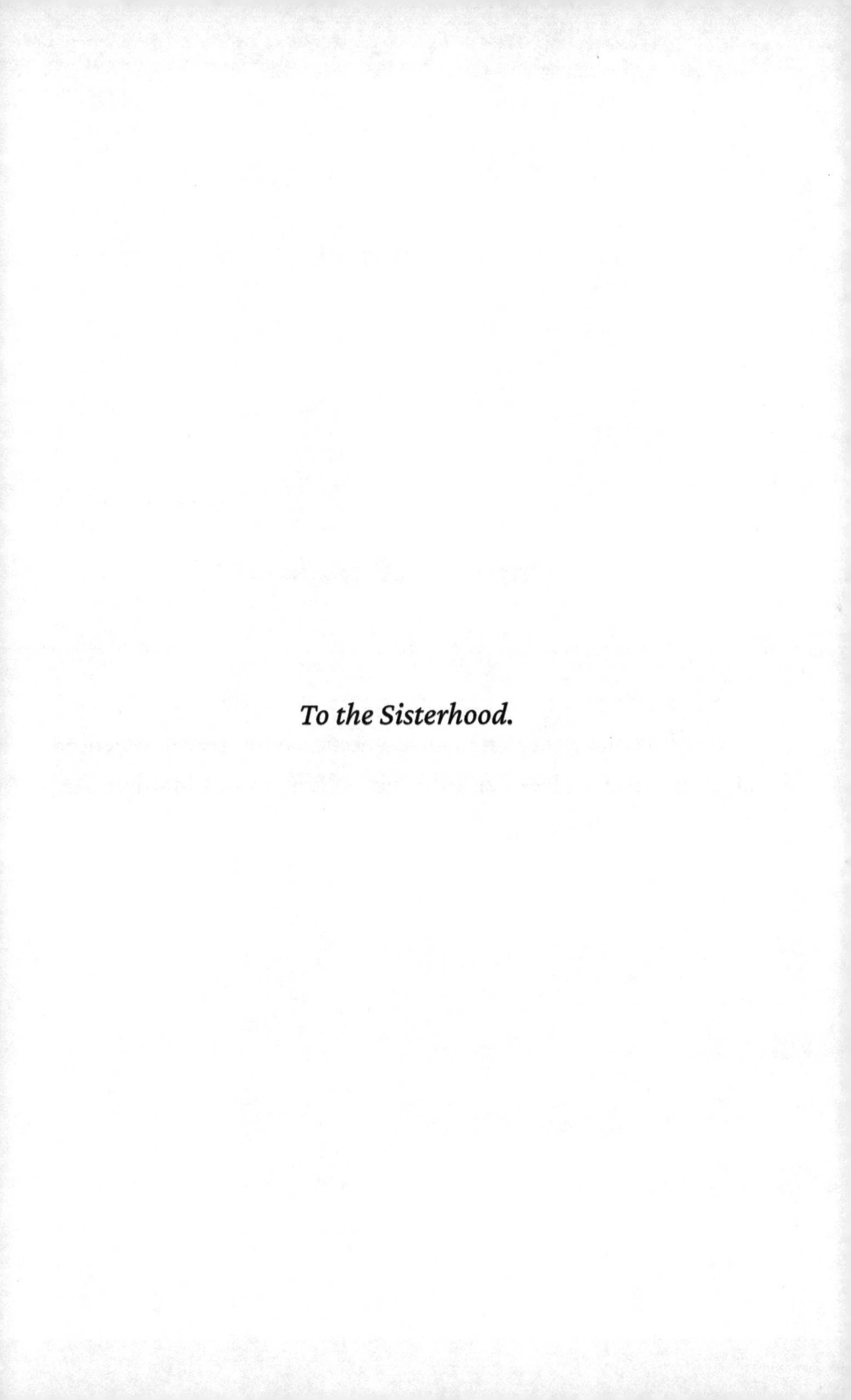

To the Sisterhood.

Content Warning

The stories in this book explores aspects of patriarchy and misogyny and contains depiction of domestic abuse, sexual violence, ableism, mental illness, suicide, alcoholism, and eating disorder. Please read with care.

TABLE OF CONTENTS

My mother has a scar on her left wrist—a wiggly snake-like line, crossed by shorter vertical marks, like a strand of barbwire. It's crude, this mark from hurried stitches made in urgency to save a life. When I was a child, the scar was usually hidden behind a fancy wristwatch—my mother had many such watches, often gifted by my father—but the limited mobility in her left hand was always a reminder of what was hidden.

Whatever had happened to give my mother that scar occurred when I was an infant, my sister barely two years old. Though my parents and sister remembered, they never spoke of it. It was understood that this past incident wasn't to be discussed. But members of my extended family would bring it up without directly addressing what really had happened. Like the stories of mythology and folklore that humans have shared since the beginning of time, my family transformed my mother's scar into the stuff of legend, using the mark on her wrist to explain my mom's fiery temper and personality.

"You know how your mom is. Look at what she did to herself once, so impulsive!" my aunties said.

Or, "Everyone is afraid of your mother," my grandmother

explained. "She used to yell at me for not watching you girls correctly. So aggressive and overprotective of her ugly daughters who don't even deserve such attention!"

To the outside world, my father was an intelligent, successful, and respected man who was never appreciated by his aggressive, strong-willed wife and too-smart-for-their-own-good daughters. Inside our home, he was a drunk menace, attacking his family with horrible slurs and accusations, eventually leading to explosive fights with my mother that often lasted all night.

As we grew in this environment, my sister took on the role of "hero," the protector archetype, joining our mother to fight while I withdrew. I saw my parents as monsters and my sister as a reckless rescuer who should have hidden with me instead of joining the fight. Perhaps the early trauma of the night my mother's left wrist was scarred sparked that desperate courage within my sister—motivating her to protect me from the darkest part of my family's story.

In the heat of their fights, my father often used my mother's scar as proof that she was unstable, volatile, and reckless and that he should be praised and pitied for his patience with his wife, who was simply "too much," an "evil wife." His was just one more mistelling of a story I didn't yet understand.

It wasn't until I was around thirty, years after the eventual divorce of my parents and the family's immigration to America, that I finally heard my mother's version of the story: it was her birthday, and my father came home drunk again. The abusive rants, threats, accusations; physical threats; the birthday cake smashed over her head; my mother retreating to the bathroom and feeling the shame, hopelessness, and disappointment in her post-partum body. She saw the razor on the counter, then . . . nothing. She woke up in the hospital, and there was the scar.

Hearing her version of the story as a grown woman, a feminist no less, allowed me to interpret this painful history from a different place. I suddenly saw my mother as a woman my own age, stuck in an unhappy marriage with two little kids, struggling to do her best with the limited choices of a country and culture—1970s and 1980s Korea—that couldn't have been very hospitable to a divorced single mother of two children.

What would I have done if I were her then?

Perhaps my mother was not merely an irresponsible mother who wouldn't just leave her abusive husband. Perhaps she was not the mean, volatile, crazy monster that family myth had rewritten her to be, but rather just a woman in pain and struggling.

It's interesting to see how drastically different the folktale my own family tells depends on who narrates the story. Whose version holds the truth? Is it the version told by my extended family, the society we come from, and the outside world? Is it my father's? My mother's? Is it my sister and I—the children?

Is the story of my mother's scar one of a good man with an evil wife? Or is it the story of a woman struggling in an abusive and hopeless marriage? Is it a story about two girls growing up with a seemingly picture-perfect family suffering from deep secrets of alcoholism and abuse?

Does my mother's scar represent the shameful inferiority of one woman, or does it represent the resilience and healing of a survivor?

Who benefits from which version of the "truth"?

Just like my own family legend, old stories and folktales are often influenced by the societal programming of patriarchy, misogyny, and classism. Most often, the official narrator of these stories speaks from the dominant point of view—male, privileged or powerful, socially conditioned. Since ancient times, the female point of view in these stories has been silenced—discounted, rarely considered, or erased entirely, as in my own family folktale.

This is why the stories contained in this volume, each rewritten by a feminist author, are so important to share.

The stories in *Korean Folktales: Four Feminist Retellings* are not rosy, happily ending stories of girl-power feminism. Instead, each of these folktales tells a story of injustice, violence, and the harmful treatment of girls and women in Korea—stories that have been mirrored by real life for too long. Yet each of these tales was rewritten with the intention of sparking a fire within readers, inspiring fortitude and hope, and encouraging us all to continue healing and thriving.

By reexamining, reclaiming, and retelling centuries-old stories designed to program girls and women to stay small and quiet, the authors of this collection offer a template for transforming not only ancient tales but for reimagining the stories we continue to tell about girls and women in the world today. I hope, within the tales collected here, readers of this book find an invitation to challenge the stories of their own lives, to rewrite the legends that have never felt true, and to become the narrators that our mothers and grandmothers could have only dreamed of.

With this book, may you find the courage and empowerment to write and share the truest versions of your own folktales; may you be steadfast in honoring your truth.

Seo Choi
Publisher

INTRODUCTION

We started questioning . . .

We grew up listening to the old stories told by our mothers and grandmothers. We heard *The Tale of Shim Chong* and received the message that we must become good, devoted daughters who would heal the blindness of our fathers. We listened to *The Tale of Chunhyang* and learned to commit our bodies, our virginity, to only one man. We heard *The Tale of Kong-ji and Pat-ji* and felt the pressure that only kind, submissive, obedient daughters would be rewarded. We listened to *Sun-Nyeo and the Woodcutter* and learned that once a girl removes her clothes in front of a man, she becomes imprisoned in his world—living in his home, birthing his children, never able to return to her own self again—as if that's a happy ending.

But then, we started questioning . . .

Why are the men who show up in these stories in need of help and sympathy from their female protagonists? Why are these characters usually incompetent, maligned, abusive, or rapists? Why are all stepmothers evil? Why do daughters, after being abandoned by their fathers, offer to tolerate excruciating suffering or sacrifice their lives to either heal or save these fathers? In all folktales that end with good winning over evil, for whom is the "good" and whom the "evil"—and who determines which is which? From whose point of view are these stories of good vs. evil really told?

Those of us who have awakened to over 5000 years of inequality, misogyny, and discrimination against Korean women started looking at these old folktales with a new set of eyes and realized we must rewrite these stories from a new perspective. Once we began examining well-known Korean folktales from the point of view of women, many things changed. When retold from a feminist perspective, the girls and women of these stories—powerless, long ignored, and erased—were resurrected and returned to their agency.

In this collection, feminist musician and educator Ziihiion questions the traditional version of *The Tale of Kong-Ji and Pat-ji* and instead reimagines the life of the stepmother who had to raise her own daughter, Pat-ji, as a single mom before marrying Kong-ji's father. In Ziihiion's *New Kong-ji Pat-ji,* the perfect good daughter Kong-ji shows her weak and dependent side, while the stepmother and Pat-ji transform from representations of evil into women who are driven and independent. The original story of the rivalry of good and evil between sisters changes into a tale of sisterly love and support.

In another retelling, psychotherapist and playwright Youngmi Baek-Youn reimagines the character Maya, the daughter of a heavenly maiden, as someone who represents the countless female patients she's counseled. In this open-ended courtroom trial play, the Heavenly Maiden (Sun-Nyeo) is portrayed as a courageous and resilient survivor of domestic abuse who escapes with her children from the violence of her husband, the Woodcutter.

Author Joyce Park questions why Korea's mythical creature Gumiho, the nine tailed-fox, is presented only in female form and never male, analyzing the folktale of Gumiho against the backdrop of the witch trials of European history. She creates the protagonist Myung-Hee—nicknamed Gumiho by the men of her village, who abuse and rape her because she lives with a mental disability and has no proper guardians. In her portrayal of Gumiho, Park creates a beautiful sisterhood of solidarity that any female reader can relate to, writing: "Gumiho does not exist, only the voiceless women who were accused as harshly as Gumiho."

Sunyoung Cho-Park, a self-proclaimed folklore maniac, discovered *The Tale of Strong Siblings* in her research of folklore related to the legend of Hong Kildong and the Strongchild tales. Inspired by the local legend of a fortress wall named Hong Kildong Fortress in Korea's Chungnam Province, she writes her retelling.

Virginia Woolf once imagined that Shakespeare had a sister whose talent equaled his own and wondered what her life would have been like. In doing so, she wrote *A Room of One's Own*, now a feminist classic. Woolf's prescription for women who wanted to be writers was to acquire a bit of money and room of their own, just as the authors in this collection imagine what lessons and prescriptions these retold folktales might offer women living in the 21st century.

We are thrilled to present you, the reader, with this collection of four feminist retellings of Korean classics, and in doing so, invite you to consider not only what messages these modernized folktales have to offer women today, but what stories in your own life might be long-overdue for some feminist reimagining as well. Together, let's reclaim the narratives of women the world over.

CHAPTER 1

New Kong-ji Pat-ji

written by Ziihiion
English translation by Peace Pyunghwa Lee

My birth mother fell ill and passed away by the time I was two years old. My father, who loved her dearly, turned his face away from me, saying I reminded him too much of her. His coldness broke my heart. My father was a good but incompetent man. Although hailing from a noble lineage, he lacked the means to make a living. His noble pride had prevented him from taking on work like teaching village children, which left him utterly dependent on my mother for everything. My mother's illness came from overworking her exhausted body; since giving birth to me, she'd taken on any job that came her way, from farming to sewing to helping at other people's feasts.

As soon as *Sam-Chil-Il*[1] passed, my mother strapped me on her back and asked for work from the old woman next door. The old lady dissuaded my mother, saying it was too soon to work, but my mother did not take no for an answer. My mother's labors were unceasing. It was overwhelming enough to care for a child and a

---

1) Three-Seven-Days refers to a period of 21 days when the mother and her newborn are secluded for restoration and protection.

husband, let alone provide for the family. When my mother told my father to watch me while she set the dinner table, for example, my father—the good man that he was—would *only* watch me. If I were to cry because of a wet diaper, he would freeze and urgently call for my mother, saying, "Look, the baby is crying." My mother would then have to change my diaper in another room because he was so sensitive. Indeed, my very good father would not hide his obvious discomfort, and his deeply set brows frowned until my mother carried me out of the room.

When my mother died, my father entrusted me to the granny next door. The old woman who had taken pity on my mother complained but still hugged me with her rough hands. It was certainly not an easy task for an old woman to look after a young toddler, already walking.

So when the old woman got too tired, I was sent to various neighbors and passed from one home to another at mealtimes. Consequently, even though I was just a young child who could barely say yes or no, I fumed with rage. I hated the pitying looks of adults in my neighborhood. They would click their tongues and say, "Oh, the poor thing." Yet I could hear their unspoken relief at the happier fate of their own children, making my insides wrench.

Whether it was the neighborhood girls excluding me from their play or the boys making fun of me, I would throw whatever I could grab at them if they roused my anger. I intuitively knew not to behave this way when adults were present; I only lashed out when it was just us children. I could cause a ruckus and make the others cry without being noticed by adults, and I quickly learned to maintain my two-facedness. All they saw was a poor girl who roamed from house to house.

* * *

After a while, I found that I did not want to live. Every day was filled with sorrow. My father would show up hours after the sun went down to collect me. After having spent the whole day maintaining my two faces, I would burst into tears at seeing my father. That made my father uncomfortable, so he would sigh and turn his face away with a frown. His chest looked warm, but he did not hug me; his arms looked strong but couldn't hold me. I was utterly lonely. My father was the one person in the world from whom I expected warmth and affection, but he never delivered.

One day the Next-Door Granny and I went to help work at a feast at a wealthy family's house, where we met a young mother also working there. A quiet woman, she completed many tasks with a baby strapped on her back. The old lady became curious and started asking her questions.

"Goodness, you have a newborn on your back. What's your name?"

"It's Gae-ddong,"[2] the woman replied.

"What does the baby's father do?" The old lady grabbed me, shoved me in front of the woman, and kept speaking. "The mother of this child, like you, didn't get to rest after childbirth and worked until she passed away." Next-Door Granny made a *tsk* sound.

____

2) *Dog poop.*

"Ah. . . ." The woman eyed me with sympathy.

Her situation was pitiful indeed. The man who promised to wed her turned out to be married with kids, but when she realized this, she was already with child. She tried almost everything to abort the baby: flinging herself from mountains, drinking soy sauce, and jumping into deep water, but the feisty life within her survived it all. She could not stay in her village, filled with people gossiping about the baby and its unwed mother, so she crossed to our side of the mountains and lived in a mud hut there. The old woman's eyes shined as she listened.

"The father of this child is alone after being widowed," Next-Door Granny said, gesturing to me. "Perhaps I can talk to him about you?"

The woman nodded silently.

"How about changing your name to Gwi-saeng?[3] Perhaps your life will be better than with your old name Gae-ddong."

* * *

The woman who became my stepmother was sturdily built and healthy. With her daughter Pat-ji strapped on her back and me nestled under her arm, she marched through her day. Her large hands and long muscled arms were strong, and I felt comfortable and at peace whenever I was in them. Maybe it was the new name given to her by Next-Door Granny, but my stepmother started glowing and flourished. Yet she was still quiet and reserved.

---

3)   *Precious life.*

My stepmother seemed to be gifted at bringing life to all things. She carefully tended the baby magpies that fell from a tree after losing their parents to a hawk until they could fly away on their own. The flowers in the yard that had withered after my mother's passing came back to full bloom under her care. Whether a fawn with a broken leg, a blind kitten, a dragonfly with broken wings, or a bee limping around the floor, she seemed to have this strange, magical power to heal and care for living things.

She also took care of my father with all her heart. But he was, perhaps, too heartbroken to open to her magic. Unable to heal his heart after being widowed, he was the only one my stepmother could not rejuvenate. He would frequently refuse to eat the food she so carefully prepared. But my stepmother did not complain. She would take my father's untouched rice and turn it into rice treats for young me and Pat-ji.

But I hated my incompetent father, who was floundering in sadness. I desired to be loved greatly by my father and resented that I wasn't. I worried about my stepmother being hurt by him and was consumed with fear that she would hate me and ultimately leave us. I so loved my stepmother. From her hands to her embrace, she radiated warmth. She would hold me close to her several times a day. When I woke up and felt disoriented, she held me in her arms until I became fully awake. When I made a fuss after waking from a nap, she comforted me with a loving embrace. Every night before bedtime, she embraced Pat-ji and me to soothe us after the long day we survived, singing lullabies into the night.

I behaved well out of fear that she would leave me, but sometimes that same fear would prompt me to act out. Anyone else would have been frustrated with how capricious I was, but not my stepmother. She stayed put like a giant tree, an enormous mountain that could not be moved. My broken heart started to heal. My stepmother's embrace was full of warm, magical, healing energy.

My new mother wanted to teach Pat-ji and me life skills. She made small water jugs for us so we could accompany her to fetch water from the well. When I was around six and Pat-ji around four years of age, she took us to the mountains and the fields and taught us how to identify edible plants and healing herbs. She made us little baskets to put the plants in during our outings. With her, I learned all the names of the plants and the many ways they could be used. The different tastes and scents were marvelous to discover.

While my father learned about the world by sitting in his room reading books, my stepmother learned about the world by experiencing it with her whole being and taught all she knew to Pat-ji and me. She taught us how to predict weather changes by observing insects and animals, connect to the earth by working in the fields, and appreciate even the smallest living creatures in the world. She made us child-sized tools such as little hoes and laundry bats, and we learned to do everything she did while playing house. Everything we did with her was a time to play and learn.

* * *

When I first met Pat-ji, I was nearly three years old, having passed my second birthday when she was just a year old. She liked me from the beginning. A bright smile bloomed on her face whenever she saw me. She babbled at me as she followed me everywhere in her toddle.

My heart fluttered, and I felt different from when I used to play with other children in the homes I was sent to. Even so, my longstanding anxiety and angst would sneak up when I was with Pat-ji. She was adorable but annoying at times, and it made me angry that she was my stepmother's flesh and blood.

Why are you the only true daughter? I wondered.

I found myself hating Pat-ji for reasons that were not her fault. When the adults were not looking, I would push her hard enough for her to fall backward, or while playing happily together, I would experience a fit of rage and smack her on the head. Pat-ji would cry loudly, and my stepmother would rush over in the middle of work. I couldn't tell if she knew I was being mean to Pat-ji, but she never said anything. I became anxious at her silence and started crying until she scooped both of us in her arms and soothed us. She never interrogated or blamed me for what happened. Even though she probably knew both of my faces.

I saw my quiet stepmother furious just three times. The first time was when village kids ripped the wings off dragonflies and tried to make them fight each other. Stepmother gathered all the village children and scolded them to release all the dragonflies.

"Do you know just how much love and effort the entire universe expends to bring forth a single dragonfly?" she sternly rebuked as she looked into each child's eyes. All the children froze as they only knew her as a quiet and kind village woman.

The second time I saw her anger, she found out Pat-ji had been pulling up plants and grass on her walk home. When Pat-ji was confronted for unthinkingly plucking plants, she complained, "Why are you making such a fuss over some weeds?"

Stepmother replied, "Every plant, every grass exists for a reason. Just because they are common does not mean they are lowly. All life is precious, and there should be no distinction between what is precious or base. What's most important is to have an appreciation and attention for all that lives."

The final time I witnessed my stepmother's anger was when I went to the creek where the women were doing laundry and threw large stones into the water for fun.

I did not expect a scolding when I threw the rocks into the creek. But she made the scariest face I had ever seen and asked why I'd done it.

"Just because," I whimpered. "When I do that, the other things in the water get startled and swim away, and I find that fun."

"You should never do that," she told me. "There are countless beings that live between the rocks in the stream. You may have thrown in a rock for fun, but little bugs and other forms of life could get hurt or even killed. Imagine if someone hurt or harmed us just because we are powerless, poor, and invisible."

When she put it that way, I realized my huge mistake and was overcome with fear. I started crying loudly. "What to do now, Mother? I feel so bad for the little beings underwater."

My stepmother responded, "Apologize from the deepest part of your heart and promise that you will not repeat the same mistake. Close your eyes and pray so that your heart will be felt by those little beings in the water."

I did everything she said with deep intention and sincerity. I felt like I had heard words of forgiveness from life underwater. In that way, I, Pat-ji, and the village kids were all scolded to tears. And we never did things like that again.

* * *

As I settled into life with my stepmother and Pat-ji, my shattered heart slowly recovered, and I stopped being mean to Pat-ji. I had been cruel to her, yet Pat-ji dearly loved me. We became the best of friends. Together we tackled household chores without Mother asking us. We sought a craftswoman in our village and asked her to teach us how to make a *ji-gye*, wooden carrier. The woman taught and guided us throughout the entire process, from finding suitable wood to carving and binding the pieces together to create a sturdy carrier. Thanks to her, we each had a small toy-like *ji-gye* we could strap on our backs when we went looking for firewood in the mountains.

Our grief-stricken father disapproved of our roaming the fields and mountains and now nursed a never-ending cough. "Girls should stay put and learn housework until they get married. If you keep going out and about, bad things will happen," he would croak between his coughs.

"Please don't worry," I responded. "We'll be sure to find some herbs to heal your cough." Then, holding hands, Pat-ji and I would run out of the house.

But I understood why he was so worried. There were rumors everywhere that several girls were raped in the mountains, and village folks bemoaned the plight of these girls.

"Their lives are ruined," they said. "Who will want to marry girls dirtied by rape?"

When boys in the neighborhood laughed about those girls, I became angry. But I could not say anything back because I cared about my reputation. I just fumed with rage instead. But Pat-ji, who was born just and fierce, would raise her voice and yell at them.

"You bastards, is that something to laugh about?" she shouted. "How would you feel if such terrible things happened to you and you were met with ridicule and mockery when you returned?" She even got into fistfights at times.

"Goodness, how will Pat-ji ever get married with that temperament of hers?" the village women lamented amongst themselves whenever they saw Pat-ji involved in a physical brawl with the village boys.

But Pat-ji was great at fighting. With her sturdy constitution and stamina, she was never defeated, even if she took a rough beating from the boys along the way. She was talented in physical battle, gaining many skills from what she learned by winning and losing. With each brawl, she became better and better.

One day, the boys who were beaten up by Pat-ji were seen running from her out of shame. I sometimes worried that the boys would plot revenge, but she was naturally sociable and likable and got along with them the next day.

But the awful rumors in the village had us worried. Someone needed to capture and imprison the evil man raping girls, but somehow no one thought to try to catch him. One could start tracking him by interviewing the girls he attacked.

"*Sung,*[4] why don't we start dressing up in boy's clothes when we go to the mountains? Skirts are uncomfortable, especially when fighting." Pat-ji's words made me laugh, and I quickly agreed.

"Yes, let's do that. If we wear boy's clothes and our *ji-gye* carriers, people won't know we're girls."

We became excited about putting Pat-ji's brilliant idea into action.

* * *

The next day, we wore the boys' clothes we had sewed the night before, put on our carriers, and left for the mountain. We skipped and danced our way to the mountain, naming all the plants and flowers on our way and discussing their medicinal uses. The mountain always put my heart at ease. The birds' songs from near and far made my heart flutter, and the varying scent of the trees, the plants, and the flowers each season was always delicious. I adored the smell of the wet earth on days it rained, and I loved the toasty scent of fallen leaves in the autumn. The sound of the stream calmed and comforted my saddened heart. On days I did not want to live, I would enter the mountain, and after crying for a long while, I felt as if the forest gods were comforting me. The mountain, the forest, was a safe space for me.

When we were deep into the woods, we could hear someone's voice crying out from afar. "Please help! Save me!"

Startled, we ran over to where the screams were coming from.

---

4)   A local variant of *Hyung,* to mean older brother or sibling, was also used by sisters.

An old man with a wooden carrier on his back was slumped on the ground.

"Huh, two boys with voices of girls. . . ."

The old man continued to speak. "I have not eaten for days, and I no longer have the energy to move. Could one of you escort me back to my hut?"

"Why would he ask just one of us to help him move?" Pat-ji whispered into my ear. "Something is off. Let's leave."

I also found his request strange, but I was determined to be good and thought it was the right thing to help this poor old man. I ignored Pat-ji's words because I thought a good child would help an adult in need.

"Yes, I will help," I said. "And we are girls. We are wearing boys' clothes because of all the horrible things happening in the mountains."

I took off my carrier and helped the old man stand up. "Pat-ji, wait right here. I will be right back."

"The hut isn't far," the man said. "You can help me there and come right back."

I helped the old man, ignoring Pat-ji's face that quickly turned grim. *What could happen in the middle of such a bright day?* I thought. *There is no way this kind-looking old man could do something terrible.*

I tried to erase all the doubts and uncomfortable thoughts that sprouted in my mind and focused on the fact that I was helping someone. I even felt a little smug. *I am a good girl*, I thought. I opened the entrance of the run-down wooden hut and helped the old man into the room.

"If you lift up the bed covers, there is a bowl of rice gruel," he said, rasping with a dying voice. "Would you please bring that to me? I need to quench my hunger."

As I knelt, groping for the bowl of porridge, the old man I thought was dying suddenly stood tall and pounced on me. I was too shocked to scream and resisted with all my might.

"It will be over soon if you just shut up," the old man muttered as he fumbled at my crotch. I bit down my lip with terror, shaking from head to toe. I tried to resist as much as I could; my tears kept falling.

"*Sung*! *Sung*!" I could hear Pat-ji calling for me. I screamed with all my might.

"Pat-ji! Save me!"

As the hut's door sprung open with a bang, the old man's wiggling stopped.

"Kong-ji are you okay?"

I could not answer her and could only weep.

"Come on, let me help you up. Let's leave. I would love to kill this bastard, but I don't want to become a murderer."

Pat-ji helped me escape the hut. I cannot recall how we made it back home. I think I ran, maybe I fell. I think Pat-ji kept saying to me, "It's okay now. It's okay now. I'm here now."

I passed out as soon I got home and woke up countless times, screaming from nightmares. Every time, Stepmother would hold me, and I would drift back into sleep while weeping. Pat-ji told Father and Stepmother that we should alert the authorities of what happened to me. After looking at my father, who was visibly uncomfortable with the idea, my stepmother shook her head no.

I could not leave the house for a while. I fell ill and stayed in bed for days. Every time I woke up shaking and screaming, Pat-ji fed me porridge, wiped my cold sweats, and cared for me. I lacked the energy to make it to the outhouse, so I used a chamber pot, and Pat-ji took care of even that.

"Thank you, Pat-ji," I said. "If I had only listened to you, you would not have to go through all this trouble. I am sorry."

"*Sung,* not at all. He's the evil bastard who took advantage of your kind heart," she replied. "Who can know the evil plotted by such a bad person? Please don't give it any more thought and just rest. Leave the housework to me."

But then I remembered all the cruel things I did to Pat-ji when she first came to live with me and felt deep remorse.

"Pat-ji, I used to hit and pinch you while you were young, behind Mother's back. I am so very sorry," I wailed.

"Kong-ji, I don't remember those things. I can only recall memories of you taking me here and there, playing with me, and always being there for me. You are dear to me, and I am so thankful for you."

"Oh, Pat-ji."

The bright smile radiating from her loving face both warmed and pierced my heart.

* * *

After ten days of ailment, I changed into boys' clothes and left the house with Pat-ji—unable to wear skirts any longer, I was terrified that someone would see me as a girl and assault me. Our attire became the subject of neighborhood gossip. Even village boys openly mocked us.

Every time that happened, I had to calm Pat-ji's anger.

One day, Pat-ji came back home in tears after a fight.

"Why did you fight?" I asked

"The kids were making fun of us."

"What did they say?"

Pat-ji was only silent.

"Pat-ji, tell your *sung*. What did they say?"

"They said we were probably engaged in *baen-dae-jil*."[5]

"So you just hit them?"

"It would be one thing if they made fun of me. But they were saying something about you. How could I stay quiet?" Pat-ji sank to the ground, wiping her tears with her fist.

All I could do for her was pat her shoulders. *Does she even know what sex between girls is?* I wondered. *Is she upset because she knows the meaning?*

"Pat-ji, are you worried that this is true?" I asked. "Do you even know what *baen-dae-jil* is?" She shook her head no.

"You are my most precious person, and I won't allow those jerks to badmouth you. I am going to kick their asses if they do," said Pat-ji with a scowl.

"I am so heartened by you. Thank you for looking out for me. I am grateful, Pat-ji. But I really don't want you getting hurt or being in danger. I'm worried. From now on, I will deal with those kids myself. So you just come tell me when they make trouble, okay?"

Pat-ji fell quiet for a bit as if deep in thought. She raised her head and said, "But why? I am going to protect my sister! Forever!"

---

5)   A derogatory term that mocks sex acts between women. Another similar term that describes the sex act of two women is *dae-shik*. 좋은 문장을 쓰기 위한 우리 말 풀이 사전 https://terms.naver.com/entry.naver?docId=1669557&cid=50802&categoryId=50812

"Thank you dearly, Pat-ji. You care for me so much. But can I ask that you wait to protect me until much later when you are much bigger? And only when I become so weak that I am unable to protect myself. Could you wait until then, please?"

"Fine! When I grow so strong and tall and can lift stone mortars easily, you have to tell me! Alright?"

A corner of my heart warmed. Once filled with aches and bruises and cold, lonely fear, this heart was melting with Pat-ji's love.

"Also, *sung*, at least let me teach you how to fight. Every girl needs some fighting skills."

From that day onward, Pat-ji taught me how to use my fists, swing bats, and, most importantly, scream and run away from danger.

Then, one day, Pat-ji told me, "*Sung*, if you ever want to talk about that day in the mountains, you can talk to me whenever. I will continue to listen until you start feeling better."

She was worried I was keeping it all inside and hurting all alone. Surrounded by her deep love, my heart grew stronger and healthier. While it was still hard to walk through the mountains, I no longer froze at the mere thought of them.

* * *

Father still disapproved of our unconventional ways. One day he called the elderly matchmaker to the house. I would turn fourteen in a year and was deemed ready for marriage. The matchmaker scanned me and said, "With her big buttocks and thick arms, she will bear many children and be great at housework. I will look into comparable families. But her appearance...."

Pat-ji barged in, yelling, "What's wrong with her looks? Who are you? How dare you say anything to my beautiful *sung?*"

"Goodness, what's wrong with you?" the matchmaker broke the awkward silence following Pat-ji's outburst. "Do you even want to get married? I will never serve as your matchmaker!"

"I refuse to marry! I am going to live with my sister forever! Kong-ji, don't go!" Flailing her arms and legs, Pat-ji fell to the ground and wailed.

Father, observing from a corner of the front yard, muttered, "What ridiculous behavior from a young woman. How did her mother raise her?" He asked the matchmaker to put forth a good effort and went into his room.

"Pat-ji, I am not going anywhere just yet," I said. "Don't worry."

"*Sung*, don't leave," Pat-ji sobbed, her face covered with tears. "*Sung*, I can't live without you."

"I feel the same, Pat-ji. How can I get married without you?"

I felt something fiery erupt from deep inside me. I bit into my teeth to avoid tears.

* * *

Stepmother made sure I had everything ready for married life. She brought my attention to a bundle and said, "This will especially come in handy."

When I unwrapped the bundle, I saw several cloth diapers the size of my palm. "Aren't these diapers? Since I'm still childless, I can prepare for them in due time."

"Those are *gae-jim*,"[6] Stepmother explained. "When your body is ready to bear children, you will bleed from down there. It happens monthly, so it's called *dal-geo-ri*.[7] When your menses begins, you will use these *gae-jim*. So keep them safe, and when you start seeing blood wear them inside your underpants. I am sorry I didn't teach you earlier."

"Oh, Mother. Thank you. I will keep them safe and use them then."

"Make sure to clean them with cold water as cold water rinses the blood out," Stepmother instructed. "Your belly might hurt when you have your moon time. When that happens, heat up some dried red beans, put them in a pouch, and keep your stomach warm. Mugwort is also great. Make sure to take them then. It should help."

She gripped my hand and reminded me not to forget.

* * *

On the day before my wedding, Pat-ji started crying early in the morning. Stepmother sent Pat-ji away to work for a few days at a village over the mountains, and I spent my first wedding night at home without Pat-ji, then left for my new home the next day.

After I got married, my father's illness worsened. Although he never once gave me a kind look or thoughtful words, perhaps he found comfort in my presence and was reminded of my birth

---

6) Article women wore during menstruation, often made from scrap cloth.

7) *Dal-geo-ri* literally means lunar/moon passage.

mother. Thanks to my diligent stepmother, their household was flourishing. She continued to make meals with healing herbs and cared for him with medicine obtained from the pharmacy. But father lacked any will to live and refused to open his heart to Stepmother.

Who was my stepmother to my father? I wondered.

Father was the youngest son of a crumbling noble family who had failed to obtain a government post and was living in seclusion in the countryside. He had two older brothers, both of whom passed their initial entrance examinations and managed to save their noble pride. On the other hand, my father loved singing and drawing but did not have much luck when it came to studying and could not pass even the most basic entrance exams that confer one's nobility. Thus, he had long been considered a source of family shame. But one day, a marriage proposal came through from a merchant-class family who wanted to play at being nobles.

As was the norm for everyone in those days, Father met my birth mother for the first time on their wedding day. He was twenty, marrying my mother, who was four years younger, and she appeared like a heavenly maiden to him. Father was so awkward and nervous about spending the first night with my mother that he cleared his throat and began to sing.

After he sang, he asked, "Do you have anything for me to write with?"

When my mother shook her head no, he said, "Why don't I tell you an old tale instead?" He did everything to ease the awkwardness with his beautiful bride and regaled her all night with stories he made up. Laughter was heard from the room where they spent their first night together. My mother must have delighted in his silliness.

Even when they moved into a run-down hut to begin their lives as newlyweds, my mother never complained and instead cleaned and shined their home, taking on whatever work she could find to make ends meet. She was bone tired from working relentlessly yet found comfort lying in bed at night listening to my father tell stories. Father was great at making up tales. As a merchant's daughter, my mother suggested that he write all the stories down into a book and that he might even make a fortune.

Father smiled brightly and promised, "One day, I will surely write a book."

Their deep affection was maintained even when my mother was pregnant with me. When she craved wild berries while suffering from morning sickness, Father braved the winter snow and foraged for berries. But once I was born, all of my mother's attention was directed to me. Her bosom was mine. I was always in her arms.

After that, Father felt pressured to provide for his wife and child. He got enraged at the littlest of things. Mother reassured him that she would earn money and suggested he continue to write down his fun stories, but that's when he began changing.

He'd yell at my mother, shouting that he could not focus on his book with a crying newborn, angrily leaving the house with the money he did not earn. He'd go out into town, have dinner alone, and return home when it was dark.

It was overwhelming for my mother to handle everything on her own. Even the solace she found in my father's stories was gone as Father packed up his beddings and left their bedroom, unable to stand a crying infant. My mother cried and cried.

Then, when my mother collapsed and fell into deep sickness, Father broke down and sobbed, saying he was sorry and begging her to get better. He gave what money and grains Mother had saved to a passing mendicant monk and begged him to save her. Clutching desperately at the monk's robe, Father fell to the ground sobbing. Even with his desperate pleas, my mother could not be saved. Mother gazed at me, a toddler running around her bed without a clue as to what was happening, and with the saddest eyes, let out her final breath. Father stopped crying only when relatives arrived for the funeral rites. My father should have sobbed for longer and grieved deeper. Perhaps his illness resulted from hardened grief that could not flow out as he tried to live up to the cultural norm that men should never cry.

* * *

My new husband's family was dirt poor. Like my father's family, my husband also came from a family of the noble class who failed to pass the civil entrance exams to obtain work. My husband was quiet and reserved but was not a bad person. He was renowned for being a devoted son who took great care of his mother, who had been widowed far too early and raised him on her own. As our families had arranged our marriage, his mother fell off a stone bridge and injured her leg. When we married, she was still in bed as her wound worsened, and within two months of our wedding, she passed away. We were extremely poor and had a funeral with what little we could afford. My husband, a devoted son, still vowed to complete the three-year mourning rite[8] and built a hut in front of her grave.

Although we consummated our wedding night, I was young, and my menses came later, so I became pregnant with our first child a full year after we married.

I was weeding in a field when my first menses began. When I stood after a long period of squatting to work, I felt a wave of dizziness and a dull ache in my belly. Thinking it was from constipation, I ran to the forest and lowered my underwear. Instead of poop, I felt something expel with a plop from inside me. Too shocked to properly tie my drawers, I stood up. Dark blood was inside them, and more blood was where I was squatting.

This must be it, I thought. *This must be the menses Mother told me of when she gave me the* gae-jim. I stopped working, grabbed my hoe and basket, and ran home. I rummaged through the closet and found the bundle with the neatly-piled handmade *gae-jim*. I could sense my stepmother's affection and care in the hand-sewn pads. I took a palm-sized pad, folded it well, and placed it tied with string to keep it in my underpants. Then I rinsed the bloodstained drawers in cold water.

My lower belly ached with cramps. I lit the furnace, placed a cast iron pot, and threw in dried red beans to roast. Once roasted, I scooped them out and put them in a cotton pouch. The pouch

---

8)   Three years of mourning set aside for one's parents to honor and pay respect for the gift of life. After the funeral rites, the mourning period commences in a memorial hut with morning and evening offering of food and prayer. Many covered their faces with shrouds to mark their grief when venturing outside during this time.

was warm and comforting. I entered the bedroom and lay down, thinking perhaps it was good that my husband was away undertaking the three-year mourning rite. The floor soon became warm and toasty. I placed the pouch on my stomach and fell asleep.

The next day I grabbed the underpants and the *gae-jim* and hurried to the stream to do laundry. Several women were already doing their laundry there.

"Look at this newlywed coming to wash her womanly things. You've finally started your moon time? You will become a mother soon!"

Other women were also rinsing their bloodstained *gae-jim* and underwear. I felt embarrassed somehow and shyly smiled.

"At least your mother prepared you well. When I got married, I knew absolutely nothing about moon time, so when I first saw blood, I thought I was gravely ill and sobbed and sobbed. Later when my mother-in-law realized what was happening, she prepared some pads for me. You must have a wonderful and considerate mother."

Hearing this, I could feel my stepmother's affection even more. When I returned home, I hung up the clean *gae-jim* to dry in a place no one could see.

Once my husband learned about my menses, he wanted to have sex every time he visited—even multiple times in a single night. Sex was a source of agony for me. I would freeze, remembering the time I was nearly raped in the mountain. When my husband finally stopped grunting over my corpse-like body, I was filled with relief. I yielded because I was told it was a wife's duty, but each occasion of intercourse left me in searing pain. Afterward, I'd find blood in the bedding and boiled salted water to cleanse. I became more and more afraid of my husband's touch. At some point, my menses stopped, and morning sickness took over. Pregnancy was a good excuse to avoid sex with my husband.

Like my mother and stepmother, I toiled unceasingly and saved as much money as possible. I wanted to feed my child good food and provide good clothes. I worked night and day up until I gave birth. I dreamed of expanding our house and buying land. I got acquainted with a generous old woman who introduced me to different work in the village. I'd accompany her to help cook at feasts and took on extra work sewing, farming, and even weaving cloth from hemp, ramie, and cotton to sell in the marketplace. Using the knowledge I was taught by my stepmother, I foraged medicinal herbs and sold them to the pharmacy after steaming and drying them.

My husband came home every half month while he fulfilled the three-year mourning ritual. Every time he returned, he'd look at me with contempt for how I had turned our home into a workshop. But I only thought of my baby. I often closed my eyes and called to mind my stepmother, Pat-ji, and the forest pathway we used to walk, its soft breeze and scent. I would soon be filled with a sense of calm and peace. Then the tight knots that formed from my husband's glares would unravel, allowing me to breathe.

About a month before my first child was due, Pat-ji showed up to relay the news that my father was gravely ill. I was grateful Pat-ji came to tell me and made her favorite foods of white rice, potato soup, and seasoned roots and vegetables, feeding her well. After preparing enough food to last a few days and dropping it off at my husband's mourning hut, I prepped additional food for our journey: potatoes, riceballs, and rice water for drinking. Early the next morning, Pat-ji and I left for my father's house. Since I was heavily pregnant, walking more than 12 kilometers was not easy. The weather was no longer scorching, but the sun was very hot during the day. Pat-ji would lend me her shoulder to lean on or even carry me on her back at times. Pat-ji's constitution was comparable to an average man's. She looked even bigger than some boys her age.

Although we left at dawn, it was dusk when we finally reached home. When I arrived, my father cried at seeing me. He held my hand and said: "Kong-ji, I am so sorry. I should not have treated you the way I did. I was so deep in pain that I did not pay attention to or care for you. How great it would have been for me to tell you stories that your mother loved so much. I was a heartless and incompetent father to you. I am truly sorry. I am saddened to leave before being able to meet my grandchild." He spoke weakly.

"Take good care of your stepmother," he continued. "She suffered her whole life because she married someone like me. Gwi-saeng, thanks to you, my daughter Kong-ji was raised very well. Thank you."

He turned his head to find Pat-ji. He took Pat-ji's hand and said, "Pat-ji, I leave this world without worry because I have you. Please look after your mother and sister. While we may not have a boy in this house, I always felt secure with your presence."

At long last, with his final breaths, he offered heartwarming words that touched us. With savings pooled from Stepmother, Pat-ji, and me, we were able to have a grand funeral for my father. We purchased a bright sunny plot of land in the mountains and buried him. After the funeral rites, I returned home.

Perhaps the journey had been too much on my body, for as soon as I returned home, my water broke, and I started having birthing pangs. While I could still move, I went to the old woman in the village and asked her to send for the midwife I had chosen. She told me to not worry and to heat the room, boil water, and prepare five to six clean cotton cloths. She also told me to move as much as possible until the last minute to facilitate childbirth.

I did everything she told me to, starting the fire and boiling water. I retrieved the set of newborn clothes and diapers that my stepmother had given me during my recent visit. I also prepared premium seaweed from the southern seas and the new bedding I embroidered for the baby. I also got the dried pepper, straw rope, and coal—all things a good, diligent husband might have prepared for me.

I walked about our yard talking to my baby until the time between contractions shortened.

To ensure my baby would feel at home in her surroundings, I talked about everything I could see: the landscape before my eyes, the flowers in bloom this season, and the birds and animals visiting our yard.

The midwife arrived, along with the neighboring old woman. They told me that simply lying down doesn't help and to push while pulling on the long cloth they hung from the ceiling. I thought it might take a long time since it was my first baby, but perhaps all the moving around helped because the baby's first cry was heard following the rooster call signaling dawn.

"Your first child is a daughter. Don't be disappointed since daughters are great domestic workers."

"How can you call her that...." I said.

That was how my daughter, whose very presence is precious, the most beloved being in my life, was born. I sought to love and serve her the same way my stepmother loved me, like an unshakable, sheltering tree.

When I woke up to the sound of the baby crying, I could smell the fragrance of rice being cooked and seaweed soup boiling. I was overjoyed to see Pat-ji enter the room.

"*Sung,* are you awake? Mother is cooking for you. She made a big pot of seaweed soup, so I'll bring it inside soon. Do you want to try feeding the baby?"

My body did not feel like it belonged to me. I gave my aching, swollen breasts to my daughter, but the baby just cried, unable to suckle. She seemed so tiny. A newborn, only a few hours old, looked more like a hairless animal than a human baby. I knew in my mind that she was my most precious baby, but at the same time, I was terrified that I might make a mistake and break this tiny being. To think this life was in my hands, I felt so helpless and weak looking at the small creature, crying out in hunger but unable to suckle.

"*Sung,* it's hard at first. Mother said it's normal. She said to keep trying. The baby needs time to adjust too."

I straightened myself at Pat-ji's words, grabbing my breast and nudging my nipple into the baby's mouth.

Please suckle. Please. Maybe my daughter heard my desperate thoughts because she started suckling. After a few hard suckles, milk seemed to flow, and her face relaxed. How miraculous that this tiny thing could be so expressive!

---

* * *

Pat-ji and Stepmother stayed at my house for *Sam-Chil-Il* to help me recover from childbirth. Perhaps my husband heard I bore a daughter because he didn't return home even after a fortnight. I wondered how he was feeding himself and asked Pat-ji to check on him. And even if she might have found it cumbersome, she never complained and brought food to his hut every day.

One day, I said, "Pat-ji, isn't it time for you to start looking to marry?" I sounded like one of those old women in town, saying things I did not truly mean.

"Kong-ji, are you worried that I will grow old alone? Do you want me to get married, have a husband and babies, and live happily ever after?"

"Well, sure. We don't know how much longer Mother will be around. . . ."

"*Sung,* I really don't think I can marry," Pat-ji said. "The mere thought of men enrages me. Even that bastard who tried to rape you seemed fine on the outside. I like how my life is right now. I only wish we lived closer, but one day when Mother passes, I will move closer to you. I am going to entrust myself to you."

I felt at ease. I might have even smiled a little. I could not imagine life without Pat-ji. *Why can't things always be like this? I thought. We would be so happy, the three of us and my baby girl. Why couldn't we live that way. . . . Why?*

* * *

They say it's raising the child, not birthing, that strengthens love. Through breastfeeding, changing diapers, bathing, putting her to sleep, and looking at her beautiful sleeping smile, I became more enamored with my baby and gradually shed my fear and worry. Seeing her blossom and get chubbier each day, learning to soothe and comfort her as she cried, examining her poop, and being concerned about her health, in the act of caring for her she became my dearest, the most important presence in my life. I wonder if my stepmother felt the same when caring for me.

"Shouldn't we have the baby's name by now?" Pat-ji and Stepmother asked. "When is your husband coming home?"

"He probably won't be home until the end of the month. I have a name in mind. Since she's a bundle of blessings, I want to call her Bok-dong."[9]

Stepmother and I both liked the name. While people intentionally used lowly names for their beloved babies, I did not want to call my precious daughter Gae-ddong.[10] It was the same way for my name, Kong-ji, and Pat-ji's as well. While *kong* (bean) and *pat* (red bean) are both precious, I disliked having that name.

My blessed life's biggest blessing: Bok-dong. After the 21 days of *Sam-Chil-Il* passed, Stepmother and Pat-ji returned home—but only after Stepmother prepared a mountain of dried mushrooms and veggies and strung up clusters of drying persimmons to be enjoyed for months to come. Pat-ji also went to the mountains and brought back piles of firewood for the coming winter. Just being

---

9)　*Blessing.*

10)　The culture of naming and the practice of deliberately calling a child by a worthless or derogatory name was thought to protect them from evil spirits and harm.

surrounded by all this bounty made me feel warm and full. It was a sad goodbye after a time of such deep joy and peace.

"*Sung,* I will be back frequently. I will watch my niece and help around the house. I know my brother-in-law still has a long way to go before he completes the three-year-rite."

"Thank you, Pat-ji. Please look after Mother on your return journey."

The house felt utterly empty after they departed. Perhaps saying goodbye to Grandma and Auntie was sad for Bok-dong, too, as she wailed and wailed after them.

My husband abruptly returned before a fortnight had passed. He didn't even bother to look at our baby before pushing me into a corner and grabbing my waist. I knew what his body was telling me.

"My body has not yet recovered. Could we wait until I am . . ."

He erupted angrily before I finished speaking. "We need a son to carry my family line. Look how frigid you are! No wonder we don't have a son."

He rummaged through the dresser, grabbed some money, and stormed out of the house. Bok-dong started crying at the commotion. A son to carry his family line . . .

* * *

My husband did not come home until long after Bok-dong was born. Even Bok-dong's *dol*—her first birthday feast—celebrated with rice cake and other special foods made by Stepmother was carried out with just the four of us. Honey cake, snow-white rice cake, white rice, noodles, and fruit were placed on a round table with a red tablecloth: a complete feast. Bok-dong grabbed the writing brush for her *Doljabi*,[11] and I wondered what kind of person she would become. We shared our feast with the midwife and the old woman who helped with childbirth, and rice cakes were shared with neighbors as we asked them to bless Bok-dong. I also brought food in a basket to visit the hut with Bok-dong on my back. My husband was absent. I left the food in the hut and returned home.

On my way home, a neighboring woman approached me with a concerned look. "It seems your husband is frequenting a village tavern," she told me. "There's a lot of gambling going on there…I caught my husband frequenting that place and ensured he learned his lesson. You should crack down on him."

Gambling? How could a devoted son in a three-year mourning rite dare gamble?

A few days after I heard the neighbor's concern, my husband came home.

"Now that her first birthday has passed, your body is fully recovered?" he asked. "When are you going to give me a son?"

Worried his loud voice would wake up Bok-dong, I laid down quietly. "Please mind the sleeping baby."

He tossed and turned a few times, then fell asleep, loudly snoring.

After that, my husband finally returned home, having completed the three-year mourning rite. Even though he returned, he spent many nights out of the house—probably gambling. Our

---

11)   *Doljabi* — a first birthday fortune telling ritual where objects like a writing brush, coin, rice, arrow, thread and such are laid on the table for the baby to grab. The object the baby grabs is used to foretell the child's future work.

savings were being drained. Even the silver spoon and chopstick set Pat-ji gifted us for Bok-dong's first birthday present had disappeared from the cedar chest.

I soon became pregnant with my second baby. Seeing my growing belly, the women in my village grew excited and happy because they said I was shaping up to look like I carried a boy inside. But I did not want to hear such things, so I cut them off.

"Look, the baby can hear everything," I said. "I'm content with either gender."

While pregnant and raising Bok-dong on my own, I managed to build a decent tile-roofed home and bought land to farm. A shed was built, and I filled it with our harvest of rice and grains; the front and back yard were filled with blossoming flowers year-round.

Bok-dong loved drawing in our yard. After observing butterflies fluttering around, she drew them with a pebble on the ground. One glimpse of a bird sitting on a tree was enough for her to draw on her canvas of dirt yard, a stone for a brush. These were peaceful, happy days. It was my greatest joy to see Bok-dong playing in our yard. But as my days filled with peace, my husband went further astray. He frequently forced himself on me even as my belly grew. It was during this time that he became physically violent when I resisted his sexual advances.

* * *

My second child was also a daughter. As I was recovering in bed, my drunk husband barged in, screaming. "How long will you just lay there like a corpse? Give me my money!"

My oldest, who was now three, burst into tears.

"Why do you need the money? For what?"

There was no point in asking. I knew he had fallen deep into gambling.

"How dare you talk back to your husband, your master?" he shouted. "Don't think you're better than me now that you've made some money. A man needs some cash to hold his head high at the gambling parlor. Where's my money? You're not even a proper wife. You've only given birth to useless girls like yourself."

He pulled my blanket off and started kicking me. I was terrified my newborn might be hurt, so I held her deep in my embrace while being kicked. *Oh dear*, I thought. *Pat-ji is coming tomorrow. I can't let her see me hurt.*

Perhaps kicking me wasn't enough because he grabbed me by my hair, dragged me out to the yard, and threw me down. My newborn slipped from my embrace and fell into a corner, shrieking. My husband continued to beat me, and I lost consciousness.

"*Aigo*! Hey, look here! Can you wake up? What's all this mess?" The neighboring old lady shook me to consciousness. "I ran over at the commotion—things crashing and the baby shrieking—and found you like this."

After seeing that I was awake, she retrieved my newborn.

"*Aigo* . . . This poor baby! It's good earning money and all, but you should always mind your husband," she cautioned. "I knew something like this was going to happen. A woman should never seem better than her man. You should give in to your husband and let him win. Look, try to get up. Let's get you inside the room." She helped me up and led me to my room.

"How is my baby?"

"Her forehead is a bit bruised, but she seems fine."

"*Umma*?" Just then, my Bok-dong, trembling in the corner of the room, walked towards me, crying.

"*Umma*'s okay. Please don't cry. You must have worried."

"I made some barley porridge, so please eat and gather your strength," the old woman said. "I'm sorry, I only have barley."

"Thank you so much. I appreciate it."

She handed me a spoon, and I took a spoonful into my mouth. I felt searing pain; perhaps the inside of my mouth was torn.

* * *

The next day, a voice called out from our yard. "*Sung*, I'm here! Your Pat-ji is here!"

"Oh, you've arrived!" I greeted my sister.

I could not stand, so I slid the door open while lying down.

"What happened to your face?!" she asked.

"I just fell down," I quickly lied. "I tripped on the doorway on my way to the bathroom."

"No, don't lie to me. He did this, didn't he?" she said knowingly. "He beats you now? Only mere days after you've given birth?"

As Pat-ji's voice grew louder, my babies started crying.

"Pat-ji, can you please soothe my children? I'm feeling too weak."

"Ah . . . Kong-ji. I'm so sorry. It must be so hard for you. And the poor babies. Oh, dearies, Auntie is so very sorry. Come here."

"*Imo*!"

Bok-dong ran towards Pat-ji and jumped into her arms. My oldest adored her aunt. She loved that Pat-ji took her to the mountains and fields, ran around, and played with her, so she always eagerly awaited Pat-ji's visits. How shocked she must have been at hearing her auntie yelling as soon as she arrived.

"*Imo* is sorry, poor baby. You must have been scared. What can I do?"

"*Imo*, I want a ride on your shoulders!"

Because of her big stature, riding on Pat-ji's shoulders might even have allowed her to glimpse past the river into the neighboring village.

"Should we? Okay, Auntie will carry you on my shoulders! Let's go!" Pat-ji said. "*Sung*, I'm going to go out to play with her, so please eat the food I brought. Mother made a whole feast for you."

Oh, Mother, my saving grace. My mouth that moments earlier was dry as the desert started watering. How was she able to prepare such lavish food with her modest means? As I ate chopsticks full of *japchae* noodles, tears started falling. After my mother passed away, my father and I were always hungry, and even the cold rice he brought home from the village felt like a treat. But when stepmother came into our lives, everything changed. She worked night and day because we didn't have much, but with the money she earned, she fed Pat-ji and me well. She sat us around the table and, like a mother bird feeding her brood, fed us equally. When we could feed ourselves, she divided the food equally among us.

How grateful I am for her, never once feeling that my stepmother preferred her biological daughter Pat-ji over me. When we fought on occasion, she scolded us both; when one of us did something praiseworthy, she rewarded us equally. She was always consistently kind and as trustworthy as a big sturdy tree. I missed her more than my own birth mother. I thought about how lonely she must be after Father's passing, even if he was a ghost of a husband, and was struck by a deep will to live. I stuffed my mouth with rice and other dishes.

* * *

"Please forgive me just once. It was because I was drunk." My husband came home a few nights later, making excuses and asking for forgiveness. But something had snapped inside me. I turned cold.

I opened my eyes wide and stared back at my husband. "No. I cannot forgive you," I said in a low voice. "You have terrorized my precious daughters and mocked this life I created with my blood, sweat, and tears. I am going to take my money and leave this marriage. Do you hear me?"

"What, bitch?" my husband grew indignant. "You've finally gone mad. Spewing bullshit with your dirty lips. Where do you think you will go? And how is it *your* money? You show not an ounce of gratitude for the man who took in such an ugly and fat wife."

As he was about to swing his fist, the door flung open, and Pat-ji barged in carrying a large stone mortar over her head.

"You worthless scum! Are you trying to beat Kong-ji again?" she shouted. "Do I need to smash this mortar on your head for you to finally stop?"

Frightened that giant-like Pat-ji would indeed smash his head to smithereens, my husband made a hasty retreat.

"If you're ever in my sight again, I will kill you!" she screamed after him as he bolted out the door like lightning. I unclenched my own rage-filled fist and sobbed, running into Pat-ji's embrace. She put down the mortar and hugged me close.

"*Sung,* it's okay now."

This warmth. I have longed for such warmth my whole life and found it in Pat-ji's embrace.

"Yes, I'm okay. But I'm not going to take it anymore. I am going to get stronger. I will fight."

After my husband fled, my stepmother and Pat-ji moved in. Our old house was entrusted to the next-door neighbor to be used as a safehouse for poor young mothers and children who had no place to go, like my stepmother and Pat-ji long ago. It became a sanctuary for women to live and raise their children together, gathering the strength to get back on their feet.

My stepmother and I opened a shop in the marketplace. We gathered and dried medicinal herbs and roasted them, even growing some of them ourselves. We sold these herbs, and our shop soon became a medicinal tea shop, also serving healing teas.

The medicine tea shop became renowned, and we even had regular customers who traveled from afar to visit us. With the money we earned, we helped support the women and children living in our old house. Mothers with older children were even given training to work at the shop, learning about different medicinal herbs and studying how to combine and mix them and brew them into healing teas.

Pat-ji gathered the young girls and taught them physical training. By imparting valuable skills like running, transporting things with wooden *ji-gye*, using axes, and learning self-defense and fighting skills, she ensured that women could live independently. All of us—Pat-ji, me, my stepmother, the village grandmothers, and wives—came together to ensure that my two baby girls would inherit a brighter world. We carried on building this new world together, one day at a time.

About Ziihiion.

Born in the middle of the night on the Year of the Ox, Ziihiion is a feminist whose pace in life is slower and more deliberate, directed towards fulfilling all of her life's desires. She loves great stories and delights in creating and sharing her own. She researches youth and young adult culture in order to deepen feminist education and, through her work in alternative schools, is nurturing the next generation of feminist youths. She also sings as a feminist musician and served as the first secretary general of the Women's Party in South Korea.

*the Story of the Feminist who
Rewrote the Story*

Kong-ji, Pat-ji, and Me

In the original folktale, Kong-ji is described as follows:
A woman of great beauty and utterly devoted to her father, she is a paragon of virtue and diligence whose actions and discernment were faultless.

The same could be said for Cinderella, Snow White, and Shim Chong. They are all beautiful, good-natured, and love their fathers. Unfortunately, they all lose their mothers early in life. Their greatest tragedy results from the suffering incurred in a new blended family when their fathers marry new wives.

In the original folktale, Kong-ji suffers much because of difficulties created by her stepmother and stepsister, but she is unable to resolve any challenges on her own. Whenever she cries, she is helped by the likes of a cow, a toad, a sparrow, a weaver, and others.

Motherless Kong-ji probably received breastmilk from wet nurses who took pity on the widower father grieving his dead wife, and until she reached the age of running a household on her own—her teens—she was likely a recipient of village support and care. She must have received great care and welcome from her village, allowing her to grow up good-natured.

This beloved Kong-ji experiences so much grief, for the first time, from her stepmother and stepsister, who despise her. When she can finally attend a feast against all odds, she unluckily loses her beautiful flower shoe on the way. Still, with great luck, she ends up becoming the second wife of Governor Kim, whose fetish led to an obsessive search for the shoe's owner. Yet even this luck quickly fades.

Kong-ji is murdered by Pat-ji, and she becomes a ghost. Even as a ghost, she cannot or will not exercise any power; instead of haunting and tormenting all those who have wronged her as a grudge-bearing super ghost, she just cries helplessly, only knowing how to bemoan and resent.

How Pat-ji was depicted:

Bad-natured and even uglier on the outside, she was malicious, capricious, and vicious beyond words.

Pat-ji is lacking in both inner and outer beauty—not just lacking but wicked and vicious. Is Pat-ji's evil inherited through her genes? Since her mother was wicked, should we assume Pat-ji was a product of her mother? How evil does one have to be to murder one's own stepsister in order to take her place as the wife of a powerful governor?

I imagine what life must have been like for widowed Ms. Bae (the stepmother) and fatherless Pat-ji. People in their village probably did not look kindly upon Ms. Bae. By married women, she was perceived as an evil woman plotting to steal their husbands, while for men in the village, she was a temptress awaiting the caresses of a man. Ms. Bae cannot provide for herself or her daughter on her own, and in the hopes of protecting them both, she struggles mightily to remarry to survive patriarchal society.

Pat-ji is no different. Having grown up fatherless and the subject of village bullying and mockery, she tries her best to escape her lot in life by turning to trickery and becoming as strategic as possible to preserve herself and her mother. Unfortunately, Pat-ji's strategy amounted to stealing another woman's place in society, and that woman was nonetheless than Kong-ji, her stepsister. What were women's lives like during those times? Lacking male protection, women's very survival was at stake. Given this context, perhaps Pat-ji can be viewed as someone who did her utmost and sought to reverse her cruel fate.

Furthermore, what kind of ending does Pat-ji meet? For murdering her stepsister, taking her place, and deceiving Governor Kim, she receives the cruelest and most gruesome punishment: being beaten with tens of thousands of blows until her body is shattered to pieces.

I have not seen men who have raped and murdered women receive this kind of punishment in other folklore or myths. So why is the punishment so much harsher on women? What a double standard . . .

Gods do not have daughters[12]

Ovid's *Metamorphoses* contains a story of two sisters in ancient Athens, Procne and Philomela. Philomela is kidnapped by her sister Procne's husband, King Tereus of Thrace, and after being raped and having her tongue cut off by him, she is imprisoned in a stone hut on a mountain. In order to tell her horrible story to her sister, Philomela weaves a tapestry with purple threads that tells her story in writing. After receiving the tapestry woven with

---

12)   Andrea Dworkin's *Mercy* translated into Korean with the title "God is daughterless."

her younger sister's horrific tale, Procne kills Tereus' son—her own son—and cooks him over a fire, serving his flesh to Tereus.

The ending I yearned for was for Procne and Philomela to kill Tereus, but that is not how the story ends. When Tereus learns the truth, he becomes outraged and chases the two sisters that killed his son, but the gods take pity on the sisters and turn them into a nightingale and a swallow and Tereus into a hawk. Even the gods seem to be on Tereus' side. A kidnapping rapist, a mutilator of a woman's body, becomes a fearsome predator. Tereus should have received tens of thousands of blows and had his body ripped to pieces. But as the title of feminist author Andrea Dworkin's book *Mercy* says, when translated into Korean, "God is daughterless."

Pat-ji gradually warped because of the discrimination and exclusion she experienced at the hands of her village and the larger society as a fatherless child, as opposed to Kong-ji, who was embraced and treated with compassion. Perhaps Pat-ji was mistreated because of her ugliness. Pat-ji may have been a naturally cheerful and broad-minded tomboy.

Contrary to Kong-ji, Pat-ji lacked those traits deemed valuable in girls, so she existed outside the confines of patriarchy: she was Pat-ji, the "non-girl." Failing to fit into a male-centered order, Pat-ji is treated as a nuisance and rendered unlovable, a pitiable being indeed. Writing about Pat-ji, I find myself tearing up as if I were writing about my own situation. Was it so necessary to place another girl, an ugly and vicious Pat-ji, to serve as a counterpoint to Kong-ji's beauty and kindness? It weighs heavily when I wonder how many children will take divisive thinking for granted and continue to see the world in such a dualistic perspective.

Ms. Bae, the stepmother, is described as a "naturally treacherous and vicious person who wants to torment Kong-ji by any means necessary." Is it just a coincidence that such a bad-natured, evil woman becomes a stepmother? The mothers who pass away early in life are generally depicted as beautiful and kind as angels, but they often die soon after childbirth without actually raising their children, while the stepmothers who step in to raise and care for the child are often rendered "evil." Is it possible that all stepmothers around the world are so evil? Is there a special school that trains evil stepmothers? A how-to guide for evil stepmothers? How frustrating. When I was young, I wrongly thought that the character for the term stepmother *gye-mo* used the same "*gye*" as in *gan-gye,* which means to be devious and scheming. *Stepmother* became synonymous with *bad* mother. I found some comfort there because at least my mother was my real mother.

Kong-ji's Sole Support, Man-choon Choi

After marrying a widow named Bae, he handed over all household responsibilities, big and small, to her and lived cluelessly as to what was going on at home.

It is said that he begged for breastmilk for his infant child from nursing mothers. Babies start solids when they are one, yet this father begged for breastmilk for two years. Goes to show how little he knows about child-rearing. He remarries the widow Bae when Kong-ji turns fourteen. Why? The child is now old enough to be married, and it's not like little Kong-ji needs someone to look after her, so why bother with a new marriage and all? Isn't it because after his daughter marries, he would have no one to help him with his clothes and serve him meals? Apparently, Man-choon, Kong-ji's father, was so happy after he remarried that he entrusted all household responsibilities to Bae. What kind of happiness is that? The happiness of sex? The happiness at being served delicious meals? Did it not matter that his precious Kong-ji was suffering alone as long as his body and mouth were satisfied? While the stepmother abused his daughter physically and emotionally, the father sat on his hands and did nothing in response. His only concern was that his meal train might run out.

The more I think about Man-choon, the angrier I get. How come no one held Man-choon responsible for all the abuse Kong-ji suffered? Because of this long-held history of patriarchy, mothers and stepmothers are held accountable for current domestic violence. Not to mention Man-choon finds himself in a "wretched plight" when Bae abandons him after Kong-ji gets married. After Kong-ji returns from death, she and her governor husband find pitiable Man-choon a new wife who is virtuous, and they are said to have had kids and lived happily ever after. Aha! The readers are supposed to identify themselves with Man-choon. If so, there is no reason for discomfort in this story.

While this story used to be a folktale, it was probably written as a novel so that people could live vicariously through Kong-ji and forget about their own hard, complicated lives. This novel is understood to reflect common folk's deep desire that good be rewarded and evil be punished and their simple wish for happy lives. Suppose one learns from this story that good is encouraged and evil punished?

What is good, and what is evil?

What is certain is that in the original story, the readers can only see "what is good for Man-choon." Kong-ji, who represents goodness, is weak and dependent, while Pat-ji and Stepmother, who represent evil, are proactive and independent. Bae and Pat-ji demonstrate the solidarity of the mother-daughter relationship and that of other connections between women. To whom are they "good" or "evil"? As a feminist in the 21st century, this is how I would like to read the story. "Evil" is the patriarchy and the double standards that are applied differently to different genders to uphold the social order. As to what is good about the patriarchy . . . well . . . nothing.

If someone finds what is good, please inform me.

The girls, women, and daughters starring in the folktales my grandmother told me were exposed to so much danger, like the *Story of Arang* which was told differently each time. The folk story of *Arang* is a legend from Miryang of Kyungnam province. The story tells of Arang, the daughter of a magistrate of Miryang, who is tricked by a lower-class man (perhaps a stalker?) and almost raped in a bamboo forest, ultimately killed while resisting. She becomes a vindictive ghost, and every time a new magistrate is posted there, she haunts the magistrate and asks for vengeance. For a ghost who bears a grudge, she is utterly helpless. All she can manage to do is just weep and cry in front of the magistrate, similar to the original Kong-ji.

Women are written so very harmless, even as vengeful ghosts, unable to haunt or kill even a rapist murderer. Of course, the magistrates are so fragile and frightened that they die at the mere sight of Arang or upon hearing her cries. (Why doesn't she haunt the criminal herself? Why appeal to a man with social status and power to carry out justice?) As all the magistrates die, no one wants to be assigned to the town of Miryang, to the point that the village has to recruit someone brave. (There must have been appropriate criteria for appointing provincial governors.) A brave man is selected, and he survives this time with the weeping Arang, catches the criminal, and Arang's bitterness and sorrow are soothed by a shamanic ritual performed for her spirit. But he spares the criminal from death by ten thousand beatings and having his flesh pickled and sent to his mother.[13]

Hearing this story growing up, I developed a fear of being raped. There are different versions, but in some, Arang kills herself to avoid being raped. Hearing such stories, I thought: *dying is better than being raped.* Whenever *eunjangdo* (a small silver knife) appeared on TV series like *Korean Ghost Stories*, I wondered, *could such a tiny blade work for suicide?* But one naturally comes up with more effective ways to commit suicide. Most of the women in folktales have such tragic and precarious lives, and since men were both oppressors and saviors, as a young girl, I fell into deep despair, thinking no one could protect me. A woman's existence is dangerous and precarious, and she cannot protect herself. That is the reality.

---

13)   Unlike the conclusion to *The Legend of Kong-ji Pat-ji.* Pat-ji is eviscerated by beatings and her pickled remains sent to her mother.

A story of sisterly love that transcends good and evil

In this retelling of *Kong-ji Pat-ji*, the basic foundation was untouched. The characters include a motherless Kong-ji, Stepmother, and Pat-ji, while Kong-ji's father remains indifferent to home matters. However, Kong-ji and Pat-ji, originally placed as counterpoints of good and evil, were written to cherish and love one another. The binary of "good" birthmother and "evil" step-mother was also scrapped. I wanted to show, in great length and depth, how women helped one another. The story continues to subvert the binary structure of good and evil.

When I started school, it was during a time when elementary schools were called "citizen schools." The school was a kilometer walk from my house—about a 15-minute walk—but a long, long walk for an eight-year-old. When I enrolled, the number of students was large, and the school was small, so we had an average of 65 students per class and a total of 12 classrooms that were divided into morning and afternoon classes. Concerned about the long commute for fresh first graders, the school paired first and sixth graders together. My sixth-grade partner waited for me in front of my classroom at the end of each school day. When I think about it now, I am not sure how this was possible. When I finished morning classes, the sixth-grade class hadn't finished yet, and it would have been too late when my afternoon classes were over. My introduction to and commute with the sixth-grader girl was like a gift for a lonesome only child like me who had no siblings.

One might wonder how much an eight-year-old would have to say, but since I grew up alone and was quite precocious, the older girl and I talked much and got along well. After my first year, she graduated and enrolled in middle school. She must have cared quite a bit, as she would send me letters through her younger sibling and even come over to my house while wearing her middle school uniforms. While I no longer remember her name, I clearly remember how much I loved her. Whether in the past or now, I am unsure if I reciprocated or responded to the love I received. Writing about *Kong-ji Pat-ji*, I remembered the memories of that older girl, those that had faded with time.

In the story, Kong-ji and Pat-ji are stepsisters just a year and a few months apart in age. When Kong-ji turns two and Pat-ji barely turns one, Stepmother marries Father. How old was stepmother Gwi-saeng? If she were fully mature for marriage, around fifteen years or so, and even past her prime, she was not older than twenty.

Gwi-saeng, who used to go by Gae-ddong (*dog poop*), became a mother of two at a young age. While her situation improved from that of having to raise a fatherless child while navigating homelessness, she was still alone, stuck with a stoic husband and a stepdaughter named Kong-ji, who is self-conscious from growing up under an indifferent father and without a mother. She feels both pity and spite against her.

While picturing Gwi-saeng, I thought of my maternal grandmother. When I was eleven months old, my father passed away in a car accident. I lived with my grandmother from six years of age, and as my primary caregiver, my grandmother refused to pity or feel sorry for me. That might have seemed cold to others, but it was not a problem for me. My grandmother treated me the same as her other grandchildren. When I did something wrong, she yelled, "I will strip you naked and throw you out," and when I got smart and talked back, she called me a "smooth operator."

Grandmother's "fair" treatment built my confidence. I made just enough trouble not to be thrown out and continued to be a smart aleck. I was a very picky eater, and whenever I had a request or craved attention, I'd refuse to eat at the dinner table and throw tantrums. My grandmother would respond, "Don't eat it if you don't want to eat," and proceeded to take away my rice bowl, soup, and silverware. At that time, I felt crushed. But her simple response was effective at making my food complaints disappear. I've observed similar cases when watching shows that offer advice on child-rearing or training domesticated dogs or cats. It was a technique my grandmother had long practiced.

I never doubted my grandmother's love for me. My grandmother, who worked as a hairdresser her entire life until she retired in her 50s, did my hair especially prettily on special occasions, allowing me the privilege of living with a top-notch hairdresser. She would heat an iron over a gas fire and roll my hair with the iron, and I'd have luxurious curls like Eliza from the animated show *Wild Rose Girl Candy*. The next day she would curl my hair inwards, and the following day, my hair was curled outwardly, and on the day after, my hair was done up in a ponytail with curly tips. I was the only grandchild who got to enjoy this special treatment. My grandmother was proud that she was a great hairdresser and businesswoman.

While my grandmother dropped out of elementary school due to family circumstances, she was never ashamed in front of her children, who were well-educated and graduated from prestigious institutions—in fact, she was proud. Grandma gained knowledge through books, newspapers, and movies that school couldn't give her. But above all, what made my grandmother so remarkable was her wisdom and openness to new things. I discovered a healthy femininity in my grandmother's self-confidence and tried to emulate her. It naturally melted into me.

The fried tofu rice rolls she packed for me on field trips were yet another token of her love. At that time, you couldn't buy pre-made fried tofu skins in markets; they were extremely troublesome to make. It was a complicated process that involved scalding fried tofu to drain the oil, cooking it in soy sauce, cutting it carefully into pockets, and stuffing them with sweet and sour seasoned rice carefully so as not to rip the fried tofu skin. It was a special picnic meal made with my grandmother's love and devotion. While other children were packed *kimbap*, my lunch was filled with *yubuchobap*, and I adored my grandmother-made meal. She was never a full-time housewife, yet my grandmother's food was always so delicious. Whenever I savored her delicious food, she said, "Smart people cook well."

My grandmother oversaw the preparation of meals for our large family, and under her leadership, we had a truly democratic meal. There was never gender discrimination. On days we had fish, each person received a piece of fish on their plate, and on special days when we had meat, a plate was evenly distributed in front of three or four people so it could be shared fairly. There was an order to who ate first, but there was no prearrangement as to who ate the fish's body, head, or tail. From my grandfather, the most senior of all, to me, the youngest, everyone enjoyed equal rights when it came to food. At such a table, we talked and laughed and chatted all evening. Everyone was given the right to speak. No one person dominated the conversation. These daily meal tables hosted by my grandmother taught me democracy, human rights, and feminism.

A scene I miss dearly is the lunches I spent at my great-grandmother's house with my grandmother after coming home from school. My great-grandmother lived alone in a small rowhouse on the roadside in the Seongsan neighborhood, now bustling. My independent great-grandmother tried living in her son's house for some time but declared she couldn't live there, so she arranged for a place to live alone in the neighborhood where her eldest daughter lived. I went to that house with my grand-mother almost every day. After lunch—usually steamed eggs with pollack roe or salted shrimp, or zucchini and salted shrimp soup—my great-grandmother and grandmother shared digestive medicine together and laid down side by side to chat. I used to fall asleep between the two of them, lulled by their Seoul accent. When I awoke at dusk, I would cry because I was not in a good mood, but no one told me not to cry or pampered me. They figured I didn't feel well after waking up fully and calmly patted me.

The two of them were stereotypical city girls from Seoul. They were independent women. My great-grandmother, who supported her family by running a sesame oil factory, sent my young grand-mother to apprentice in beauty schools, saying, "Women must be skilled."

"Women need to be able to support themselves. Marriage is not a must," said her daughter, my grandmother, a progressive woman who emphasized that one must bear responsibility for one's own life. In portraying Gwi-saeng and Kong-ji's birth mother, I drew from my grandmothers, who ran businesses and learned skills and worked very hard to support their families. I wanted to capture the intergenerational legacy and solidarity of these women.

I also tried to have sympathy for the character of Kong-ji's father, imagining all the reasons why his wife fell ill and died so young. A hopeless romantic with an artistic sensibility, he was incapable of managing his daily life, so he became completely dependent on his wife to make money. I wrote him as a man who does not quite fit into the man-box imposed by patriarchy but was born and raised in it and thus unable to leave; a man completely broken by his wife's passing, who ached inside and died after living a lonely life unable to open his heart to anyone because expressing emotions was not socially acceptable. I thought of him as a widowed man with a daughter, prompting the village women to take pity and rally around him, saying, "*Tsk tsk*, what can a man do alone?" Even if it were with his last breath, I wished he would make peace with his new wife, Gwi-saeng, Kong-ji, and Pat-ji. I wanted him to apologize and offer a heartfelt blessing to everyone.

Kong-ji's husband is also an incompetent and distorted character, similar to her father. Branded as a devoted son in a patriarchal system, he represses himself to fulfill the role of a filial son of an all-but-declining noble family. He ends up abandoning the family he needs to care for, hiding away from reality. He undertook a three-year mourning rite to properly grieve, but this man, who did not learn how to truly grieve, tries relieving the grief through drinking and gambling.

I see in these two men members of my own family who could not let go of their grief. While my widowed mother spent time studying abroad, I was entrusted with my father's family for a few years. There was always a thick cloud of grief at their home due to the loss of their eldest son. While things seemed ordinary and even mundane during the day, at night, my paternal grandfather, who wanted to relieve his sorrow, drank a mixture of soju and beer and would cry and get angry. Or maybe he got angry and then cried. He even cried at seeing me, saying I reminded him of his son. It was hard to tell if he was crying because he was drunk or getting drunk to cry. During that time, I wasn't fully aware of my father's death, and I thought my parents had gone to study in Germany together. I was confused and flustered by my grandfather, who cried while talking about my dad, getting angry at times and throwing things. I was about five years old, sitting next to my grandfather's drinking table, watching the whole thing. I was so very scared. My paternal grandmother would kneel as if she were to blame and just took on all of my grandfather's rage. My uncle also seemed angry all the time to me, perhaps because his grief was so deep.

All the men from my father's family were like that. They couldn't let go of their grief and were possessed by rage and hurt themselves. Living with my dad's lineage, I felt like I was Kong-ji right before she met her stepmother, Gwi-saeng. My mother lived and studied in Germany for two and a half years, while I lived like a nomad, going back and forth between my father's and my mother's families. Since I was the first grandchild to both sides of the family, I was deeply cherished. In my paternal family, my grandmother, grandfather, uncle, and aunt took care of me. In my maternal family, my grandmother, grandfather, great-grandmother, uncles, and aunts treated me like a little princess. Even though it seemed like I was surrounded by overflowing love, I felt terribly lonely. When I speak about memories of that time, people respond with "What can a four-year-old remember?" and "How could a five-year-old think that way?"

The first reason for my tears was that there was no one next to me whom I could call Mom and Dad. My cousin, who I lived with, had both mom and dad, but I lacked even one. This whole situation was unbearably sad to me. When sorrow took over, I would hide next to the cabinet in the corner of the room and sob. Even when the whole family gathered for a meal, I found it sad and cried. My mother was the only person in the family photos. I couldn't find any trace of my father. When I asked about my mother in the photo, they said she was far away in Germany, along with my father, and that they would come back by airplane. Every time an airplane passed in the sky, I would point my fingers and say that my mother was over there while missing her.

My paternal grandmother loved me so much that she did not know what to do with me. To my grandmother, I was a poor little baby who needed all the care in the world; she didn't dare skip a meal lest I fly away from lack of weight. Before I went to bed, she always told me old stories and gently patted my bare back with the palm of her hands. She used to chase me around the house with a bowl to feed me one more spoonful of rice. Since the elders in the family treated me thus, my aunts and other family members could not treat me any differently. I became a grumpy little dictator distorted by sadness and a sense of entitlement. I got so angry that I even hit my younger cousin on the head with a harmonica when the adults weren't looking. When my maternal grandmother came to collect me, I got even angrier and beat my cousin as if to show off. I was a child full of rage, hatred, and resentment.

While no one gave me reasons to feel self-conscious, I grew into an extremely watchful and anxious child—anxious and scared that I might be hated or abandoned. Remembering how I used to feel back then, I allowed Gwi-saeng to embrace the child so that my inner child could find healing in a deep, warm hug.

A smile came to my lips when I wondered what kind of child Pat-ji might have been, born and raised by a sturdy and reliable mountain of a mother like Gwi-saeng. Even though I was self-conscious and wracked with anxiety, in the arms of a Gwi-saeng-like grandmother, I became Pat-ji—one who follows Kong-ji everywhere, wanting to heal her sister's aching heart and knows how to pour her heart and soul into the person she loves.

Due to things I had no control over, I was made socially underprivileged and a minority and experienced needless loss and deprivation deep in my bones. For example, homeroom teachers came into the classroom at the beginning of each school year, made us close our eyes, and said, "Raise your hand if you don't have a father." They followed with, "Now raise your hand if you don't have a mother," to investigate students' home environment. This made everyone think that losing one's father and mother was something to be ashamed of, something that had to be hidden. The first time I experienced this inquiry, I came home and asked my mother why I didn't have a father. In my second year in the elementary school when I heard the words "you fatherless bastard" from a boy who served with me as co-moderator of class, I had no choice but to knock him down on the classroom floor and pelt him with punches. Having lived through such experiences in a patriarchal society, I carried deep depression, sadness, and anger inside me.

Both Kong-ji and Pat-ji lived inside me. I strived hard to be liked by people because of my fear of abandonment, even as I refused to tolerate injustice and fought for justice. There were times when I thought being me was enough, even if I were alone. But there were also times when having both Kong-ji and Pat-ji in one body was insufficient. When Kong-ji was almost raped in the mountains, she needed Pat-ji to open the door and rush in. She was desperate for someone to accompany her on the fearful mountain path until she felt safe on their walk together.

In this *New Kong-ji Pat-ji*, I wanted sisterhood to shine. I sincerely hoped that Kong-ji, Pat-ji, Gwi-saeng, and the village grandmothers and wives would care for, protect, heal, and revive each other. So I drew a story like that. I hope this story will offer fierce warmth to girls, women, and sisters who are overcoming hardships on their own.

CHAPTER 2

The Legend of Hong Kilyoung

written by Sunyoung Cho-Park
English translation by Kayoung Kim

A long time ago, in a little mountainside village, lived a pair of Strongchildren, a brother and sister. They each showed extraordinary strength from the time they were babies. Kildong, the brother, could break nearly anything he played with, and Kilyoung, the sister, could form and build things with any heavy, solid materials she could get her hands on. For their mother, a widow, these two children—a son who liked breaking things and a daughter who enjoyed gathering and building— were too much to handle on her own. She feared for their future with such extraordinary powers and worried whether she could raise them well.

Mother's worries grew as her children did. *How do I teach them to use their powers wisely?* she thought. Yet the villagers were excited to have not just one but two Strongchildren in their community. Every day, the entire village excitedly talked about all the wonders of the siblings' powers.

"Did you hear how eight-year-old Kildong defeated that big guy, Mandol, at a wrestling match?" one said.

"Oh really? His sister Kilyoung is not even ten-years-old, yet she dug a large cave into the mountain. I heard that it is big enough to fit fifteen men!" another boasted.

"Wow, that's impressive! I want to go see that cave," said yet another, laughing. "My goodness, between the wrestling match and the mountainside cave, we will be busy with all the entertainment!"

But these stories worried Mother, each tale growing as her children grew. Over time, the siblings became increasingly annoyed with each other—competitive and in disagreement about the best use of their exceptional strength.

"So you decided to go to the wrestling match after all, after I told you not to?" Kilyoung shouted at her brother. "Mother, Kildong won't listen to me."

"Mind your own business, sis," Kildong replied.

"The more you show off how well you can fight, the more men will try to fight you. Are you going to fight all of them?"

"If anyone wants to fight, let them! I will win them all!" Kildong boasted.

"Kildong, instead of showing off your strength, why don't you do something good with it?" his sister suggested.

"As you do, building your strange things, Kilyoung?" her brother said. "Nobody cares if you make a cave or road on the hills. People just say you are weird!"

Such arguments became frequent as time passed, and the siblings became more and more competitive. At first, their competition wasn't a big deal. Kildong was busy fighting and wrestling across other villages while Kilyoung kept herself occupied building what she thought her village needed: a new well, a bridge over the creek where women gathered to do laundry, and a small playground for children. They seldom were in the same spot. But eventually, Kildong, bored with winning every match and finding no one left who wanted to fight him, started showing off his strength by destroying the things his sister had built instead. To Kildong, his sister was the only one who truly matched him in physical strength—the one person he was never able to win over.

One day, Kilyoung built a high observation tower where visitors could see all the way to the neighboring village. The next day, Kildong, complaining that it was ugly and blocked the sunlight, destroyed it. Kilyoung was angry but then quickly became inspired by the broken tower. She gathered all the dirt and stones from the ruined tower and built a dam instead, making a large, deep reservoir. Within a few days, a beautiful pool lay in the middle of the village.

Kildong felt frustrated. Seeing his sister make an even more noticeable reservoir after he destroyed her tower, he felt a sense of despair. His thoughts began to turn obsessive; *I must win. I want to win . . .*

Driven by his desire to win, Kildong destroyed the dam, draining all the water collected. Kilyoung felt a part of her heart crumble and empty, along with the crumbled dam and empty reservoir. So she decided to transplant all the trees from the forest into the empty reservoir, making a small forest in the middle of the village.

Kildong saw the strange forest and became excited. He felt Kilyoung had finally started to pay attention to him and fight back. In response, he pulled up all the trees from their roots.

But the villagers were getting frustrated and angry with the siblings. In only a few days, the village had become a destruction site from all their showing off. The townsfolk blamed the siblings and started to ignore them. Such blatant shunning and hostility was a new experience for Kildong and Kilyoung, and they blamed each other. Mother witnessed her children blame and attack each other.

"You idiot! People could see far into the distance from my tower," Kilyoung shouted at Kildong. "Why did you break it?"

"Do you know how ugly it was in the middle of the farmland?" he replied. "You also destroyed the farm around it!"

"It was you who destroyed the farmland tearing down my tower, not me!"

"It's your fault; you chose to build the thing in the first place."

The siblings argued back and forth.

"Then what about the reservoir? Do you even know just how deep and beautiful it was?" Kilyoung cried.

"In the middle of the village? People had to walk so far trying to get to the other side. That reservoir was an inconvenience!"

"People praised me because they could now have plenty of water!"

"A bunch of bull crap," Kildong muttered.

"Why do you always ruin everything I do?" Kilyoung finally asked her brother.

"Because I am stronger and smarter than you, of course! It's about time you admit it!"

But Kilyoung refused. "I am just as strong as you! And I am much better than you, who just likes to fight and show off."

"I was just accepting the challenges offered to me. You are only a weirdo who creates things that nobody wants."

Mother could not stand any more arguments. It was one thing to tolerate the townsfolk saying bad things about her children, but watching them fight each other with such hurtful words was too much.

"Children! Please stop! I cannot endure this anymore," she cried. "Do you know how hard my days have been dealing with your fights around the village?"

The siblings looked at their mother for what felt like the first time in ages. Indeed, so busy competing with one another, it had been a long time since the siblings really saw their mother. Wherever they went, they had always been offered meals by the townsfolk. They took it for granted, thinking it was natural to merely receive people's generosity instead of feeling grateful for it. But while her children accepted these meals without a thought, Mother knew how hard it was for the villagers to make ends meet, to have a spare meal to offer.

Expressing gratitude and becoming helpful to people in return was the only way her children would truly be accepted and loved by the townsfolk. So Mother had always worked hard, trying to repay them for their generosity through her own service and work. But her children had become too powerful and created a mess she could no longer handle alone.

When the farmlands became destroyed in the sibling's fight over the tower, Mother was the first to arrive, trying to salvage the crops. When the reservoir was destroyed, and it wouldn't rain, the villagers came by in groups and complained to Mother. They asked her to please stop the siblings' fighting. They'd told her that if that wasn't possible, her family would have to leave the village. They asked her to take the Strongchildren and move far away since they no longer wanted them in their town.

Now the mountainside was bare from the siblings' repeated destruction of the forest. The village had no shade from a forest, no water from a reservoir, and no crops because of the destroyed farmland. The villagers' mere survival was in danger because of the Strong Siblings' fights. Mother would have to either stop these fights or leave the village they have lived in for a long time.

"Children, if you can determine who is stronger, will you please stop this pointless rivalry?" Mother asked in a low but determined voice.

"Kilyoung cannot possibly be stronger than me, but she wants to fight me," Kildong replied.

"All I want is to be left alone, so I can use my strength as I want—to construct things," Kilyoung said. "I don't know why Kildong wants to ruin everything I try to do."

Mother interrupted, "So then, Kildong, you want to be proven stronger than Kilyoung?"

"Yes," Kildong answered without hesitation.

"And you, Kilyoung?"

Mother needed to understand the exact reason why Kilyoung and Kildong were fighting and placing blame on one another. Kilyoung did not start the fights, but she did not yield either, and so, in Mother's eyes, it seemed that there must be something Kilyoung wanted also.

"I want Kildong to stop fighting," she said, finally, confessing the deepest thoughts she hadn't shared earlier. "He fought so many people and now is bringing the fight to me. I hate it."

"If you fight me and win, then I will stop," challenged Kildong.

Looking at her children, equally strong yet wanting completely opposite things, Mother felt responsible for the situation. This was beyond making amends with the villagers for the Strong Siblings' destruction. Now what she feared most was for her children's well-being if she did not wisely resolve this conflict between them. She decided she would use all her might to prevent any tragedy from happening.

Mother spoke, "Kilyoung, I believe you can't avoid this fight. Let me wager a bet between you two. Whoever loses this bet must accept the loss without protest and leave town. The townsfolk want this, and I am getting too old to continue managing both of you."

Mother felt so certain the situation had grown bad enough to threaten her safety and survival in the village that her worries had become far greater than her children's disappointment. She believed this was the only way to resolve their ceaseless conflict.

"I will follow whatever you command, Mother," Kilyoung voiced her commitment.

"This is good, and it is long overdue," Kildong said, excited about what he believed was his forthcoming victory.

"In that case, Kildong, you will go to the forge to make a pair of iron shoes and complete a trip to Seoul and back, wearing them," Mother explained. "You must wear the iron shoes the entire trip, as there will be footprints showing the trip has been made. Can you do that?"

"That sounds easy, Mother. I will be back within a week."

Kildong's excitement only grew at what he saw as a way to

finally beat Kilyoung—a way that his mother and all the townsfolk would see.

Mother gave Kilyoung her instructions next. "Kilyoung, you will build a fort around the mountain so the trees can safely grow again. You must finish this before Kildong returns home. You must also build a door into the fort wall so people can safely travel. Putting on the door will complete your mission."

"Yes, Mother, I am confident I can do that," Kilyoung said.

Kilyoung was grateful to her mother. Mother gave her the task of building, her favorite activity, and Kilyoung felt proud her mother would be able to watch her doing the job.

"Get started now, you two."

"Yes, ma'am!" And off they went.

Kildong made a pair of iron shoes within a day. The blacksmith complained, but because Kildong helped with the kindling, they could melt much more iron than usual. In fact, they had enough iron to make ten pairs of shoes. Even though the blacksmith was unhappy about the process, he could not deny that it was only possible to complete the job because of Kildong. He decided to share some tips about the characteristics of iron with Kildong. He reminded Kildong that since iron is cold and heavy, each step could make his feet bleed unless he protected them well. He also told Kildong that since moisture would make walking more difficult, he must be diligent about keeping the shoes dry. Kildong nodded, gathered some dry cloth to protect his feet as much as possible, put on the iron shoes, and started his journey to Seoul.

Kilyoung spent her day looking around the emptied, treeless mountain. Unlike the last time she went to the mountainside when she was too focused on competing against her brother, now she could see the land and how the trees she destroyed had protected the village, the valleys, and many animals in the forest. Seeing her damage, she couldn't wait to start building the fort walls to protect those elements standing open and defenseless. She knew that no one else could do a better job.

Mother finally got her rest. For the first time, she felt peaceful. Her son was focused on making the iron shoes, and her daughter had begun carefully observing her surroundings. The family's long, unattended house was a mess, but Mother felt such peace that she was unbothered. She couldn't remember how long it had been since she could stay home during the day.

On the second day after Mother issued her orders, Kildong left for Seoul, and Kilyoung started building the fort. Finally, the town was able to see a glimpse of the peace Mother had felt the day prior. The blacksmith made many farming tools with the iron that Kildong helped to melt, and the townsfolk were relieved to see Kilyoung making a structure to protect their village. The people could now focus on reviving their destroyed farmland. They made a temporary well and gathered rainwater.

And thus, a week passed. Contrary to what he said, Kildong had not yet returned from Seoul. At the same time, Kilyoung built the fort around the barren mountain. Now she began using sturdy wood layers to make a strong door. Mother could see the progress, even from afar, and she felt very proud of Kilyoung. As Kilyoung worked on the fort, Mother walked around and salvaged the trees that could be replanted or reused.

The whole town was returning to order at a remarkable speed

without any intervention from the mayor. People were impressed with how quickly Mother had handled the situation. Mother was there whenever people felt overwhelmed about the next steps and helped the villagers identify and prioritize the most critical tasks. Before long, the townspeople started following Mother's guidance and leadership.

In the meantime, the mayor was only focused on gathering taxes and lining his pockets with rice, grain, salt, silk, and herbs from the townsfolk, even while the town looked struck by disaster from the Strong Siblings' fights. But even he noticed that something was happening among the townsfolk. From the time he arrived in town, he had closely watched this strange family, who were very well known because of the siblings who kept making rather unique problems. In fact, there had been emergency meetings every two or three days because of Kildong or Kilyoung before their mother sent them away on their missions.

At first, the mayor was shocked and tried to devise a good solution. But because these were family "problems" and beyond his jurisdiction, he stopped thinking hard about it after a while. After all, all he really needed to do was gather taxes on time and report his findings promptly to the King.

But once the problem became too large to ignore—with the tower being built and destroyed the next day, the farms being damaged, the reservoir's construction and flooding, and a drought plaguing the town—it all seemed much more like a series of natural disasters than a family spat. The mayor couldn't believe what he was seeing. What kind of mother remains in a town where her children have caused such strife? He decided to chase them away, making one excuse after another to justify their forced departure. But, inexplicably, all the townsfolk said, "While they do such harm to our town, they also keep our town alive, so we can't chase them away."

"But isn't it a priority to keep them away so that they don't damage the town?" the mayor asked.

Still, everyone responded, "No, we cannot survive without them." Some villagers were so desperate to keep the family of Strongchildren that they kneeled, cried, and begged the mayor not to chase them away.

The mayor simply could not understand. When he looked into detail why their presence was necessary for the village, all the reasons sounded trivial: how they helped take care of a man's wife after childbirth, comforted a sick child, or gathered medicine and nursed a family to health after a contagious illness. None of these testimonials sounded important to the mayor. But somehow, whenever such needs came up, people were used to seeking out Kilyoung, Kildong, or their mother, almost out of habit. What seemed trivial to the mayor had become commonplace to the townsfolk.

Though the mayor could not understand it fully, he realized it would be difficult to make all three of them leave against the wishes of the entire town. Unhappy with the situation, he started imagining instead using the siblings' power for his own benefit.

If I must live with them, then I can use them to my benefit, he thought. If successful, he could become the most powerful mayor of all, even more powerful than the King himself! It was such a sweet idea.

But the reality was different. The siblings' power did not belong to the mayor. If anything, their powers kept causing trouble—incidents beyond his ability to handle. Most of the time, he could only sit and watch as the problems unfolded. As he realized his hopes of using their powers for his benefit were just a fantasy, he became more bitter against this family. He wanted to punish Kildong and Kilyoung for the damage they caused the village, yet he feared their powers. But he noticed their mother seemed less threatening.

One day, he called his secretary. "The town has become inhabitable because of what Kildong and Kilyoung did. I plan to have their mother made responsible for their crimes. What are your thoughts on this?"

"Sir, since Kildong and Kilyoung are both young, this could be done, except...."

"Except what? Would there be any opposition to me punishing their mother for their crimes? Tell me."

"If you punish their mother for their crimes, we don't know what Kildong and Kilyoung might do," his secretary explained. "You are right that they are like two untamed beasts; however, the whole town knows how difficult it was for their mother to raise them. We all know that both children care very deeply about their mother."

"And how exactly does that prevent me from following the law?" the mayor questioned. "I am the mayor of this town."

"The siblings will not stay quiet if their mother is being punished for what they did. If that happens, we will not be able to fight against them, no matter how many soldiers we pull on our side," the secretary continued. "Right now, they are fighting against one another, trying to prove themselves, but in case they decide to combine their strength against us . . . I do not even want to imagine what might happen in that case. Unless the case is so elevated that the King himself makes the decisions, it is my thought that punishing them will lead to more loss than gain. There isn't a specific crime to charge them with, and their mother is doing much for the town. Please consider all aspects of this case and wait for the right time to act."

The mayor knew that the secretary's recommendation was wise, well-experienced, and trustworthy, but it meant that he could not do anything immediately and angered him even more than before.

The whole town follows that mother of Strongchildren even more than my own authority, the mayor thought to himself. *How can a mere widow try to lead the people? That woman is disrespecting my authority only by the power of her children. This is a crime, and I will make her pay for it. But I will wait since I don't want to waste my soldiers on her.*

Understandably, the bet between the siblings was an excellent turn of events for the mayor, who was waiting for the opportune moment to enact his plan. Kildong had left town, and Kilyoung was confined to the mountain at the village's periphery—the mayor thought it the perfect time to act.

Of course, Mother was unaware of the evil mayor's plan. For the first time in her life, she felt safe, peaceful, and happy to think she was helpful to her town and its people. It seemed people were coming to her only yesterday to complain about her children, yet now, everyone was seeking her advice. It is said that challenges can turn into opportunities, and the challenges she had because of her unruly children suddenly became an opportunity to be more influential and valued. *No one would dare ask us to leave this town now*, she thought. The bet would continue peacefully until a clear outcome.

But all at once, Mother's face fell. One concern she couldn't shake was that she would need to permanently send one of her children away from the village. It made her sad thinking of what was to come. She had sensed that a child's separation was bound to happen someday and thought it might as well happen with the bet she proposed.

She tried imagining her life without either her son or her daughter. *Since Kildong hasn't returned yet, perhaps I will end up living with Kilyoung in the village*, she thought. *Well, that's good since it is less dangerous for a boy to survive on his own. Whatever he decides to do with his life, as long as he knows how to use his power wisely, he won't get into trouble. Maybe he'll be revered as a strong hero wherever he goes. But it wouldn't be the same for a girl like Kilyoung.*

Mother let out a sigh. It was a big relief for her to see Kilyoung progress on the fort at a fast and reliable pace.

* * *

Nearly a week after the bet was wagered, the mayor ordered the mother to be arrested. Mother, along with the other townsfolk, was dumbfounded.

"What crime do they say she committed?" wondered the people. They worried about her children hearing news of the arrest before the bet between siblings was settled. Some went to the mayor to ask.

"Mayor, the bet between Kildong and Kilyoung is not over just yet. Why did you arrest their mother?"

"A bet, you say? Are you saying that a bet is more important than carrying out official business?" the mayor replied. "Also, how dare you demand an explanation from me?"

"No, sir, it's just that the ongoing bet between her children is very important to us all."

"If so, then why didn't you report this important business to me in the first place?" the mayor challenged. The villagers didn't know how to respond.

"Sir, it's because you handle more important affairs," they finally said. "Their mother had been handling the situation quite well."

"I arrested her precisely for that reason. How dare a woman to decide to handle important business for the town? Who gave her that authority?"

The townspeople froze. They were certain that one wrong word out of their mouths would lead to their arrest too.

"Okay, sir. Please forgive us for not thinking through this," they said. "We will trust that you will enable the bet's completion."

As they left, they ran straight to Kilyoung, who was building the fort day and night in the mountain. Kilyoung was just about to choose the sturdiest wood for the door to be placed into the fort wall.

"Kilyoung! Kilyoung! Something terrible has happened," the villagers announced. "The mayor has arrested your mother."

"My mother? Whatever for?" Kilyoung asked. "She is not the type to commit any crime. I'm sure there is a misunderstanding. It is probably nothing."

Kilyoung was so focused on the last step to cement her win she didn't want any interruption.

"Kilyoung, we're telling you, this is serious," the townsfolk insisted.

Kilyoung paused suddenly as a chill ran from her elbow to her ears. She put down the wood for the door and looked at the people's faces, each full of fear.

"You have my full attention. Please tell me what is going on," she said.

At that moment, Kildong had nearly returned to town. He only had one hill left to climb but was too exhausted to continue. He sat with his eyes tearing up. He had been so confident he would complete his journey in one week. But as soon as he started, the skin on his feet broke in the iron shoes, making every step painful. Each night he needed to treat his bloodied feet with herbs and rest. It was not an easy journey to Seoul. He constantly needed to search for clean water and healing herbs to care for himself. His heavy shoes made traversing the rugged terrain difficult, and he learned that his physical strength was usually worthless.

"How useless my brute strength is," muttered Kildong. He took off the shoes to look at his bruised and abused feet. His skin and toes were damaged inside the shoes, and he felt deep sadness and regret.

"Why did I even begin this bet?" he wondered aloud. "Why did I think that I could win without any pain?"

He couldn't help but admit how foolish he had been. His poor feet seemed to blame him too. The thought of revealing this broken self to his sister felt too vulnerable. It had been over a week since the bet was waged, and he was certain that his sister had long finished the fort—she was so good at building things. Sure of his loss, he had lost all motivation to continue his journey.

"What is the use in going back like this?" he said to himself. "I already lost the bet and will only be kicked out again."

He suddenly realized that he had never imagined living without his mother or sister. He also admitted he always felt angry at Kilyoung. Unlike his mother, his sister did not love him unconditionally. She would scold him for the littlest mistakes, and she was so hard to please. Then when she started making beautiful, impressive things, he got jealous. His jealousy and resentment pushed him to destroy those beautiful things she made. For the first time, Kildong felt sorry for his actions. The years of resentment and anger did not magically disappear at once. Still, the pain in his feet reminded Kildong of childhood when his sister would comfort him with so much sweetness whenever he fell or hurt himself. He felt embarrassed at how childish he had been, being so angry at Kilyoung when all he really wanted was to be loved and approved by her.

The pain made him miss his mother too. No matter what trouble he got himself into, his mother was always there for him. If he hurt himself, she would find the medicines to heal the wounds. He imagined his mother waiting for him on the other side of the hill, regardless of who won the bet. He thought about how he had been taking his mother's love for granted while he tried to demand his sister's love to be unconditional too.

"I need to say my goodbye to them even if I end up getting kicked out right away." Kildong stood up, determined. The days of pain were felt through each toe, but somehow he felt much lighter. He was learning for the first time how soul-freeing it was to accept his own flaws.

* * *

In the nine days since the bet was waged, Kildong had not returned, and Kilyoung's fort was not completed. All the rebuilding and repairing of the town was done, and the Strongchildren were not around. The mayor thought it was the ideal time for him to take control. Feeling cocky, he accused Mother.

"You should know the crime you've committed!"

Mother felt indignant but replied calmly. "I don't believe I have committed any crime, but I understand I am partly responsible for the situation of our village."

The mayor was taken aback at her calmness and quiet strength. He had thought the Strongchildren's mother a fragile widow, but now he could see she was a remarkable woman to handle two Strongchildren and endured thriving in the village. Her strength annoyed him; he wanted to break her spirit by cornering her.

"Yes, all the damage and chaos in the village is your fault. How will you pay for your crime?"

"I cannot, sir. You are the mayor of this town; how could I dare take responsibility for the entire village?" Mother replied. "Please, reconsider."

All at once, Mother felt very tired and hopeless. She could see the mayor was set on putting the entire blame on her to punish her, and she had no power or authority to refute it. She did not even understand the motivation behind his accusation. No matter how hard she tried, she could not see a way out of her predicament. Seeing Mother's resigned expression, the mayor gleefully yelled.

"For the crime of destroying and creating chaos in our village, I will punish all three of you. Whoever loses the bet will pay with their life. That's a worthy punishment for your crime."

At this, Mother came to her senses. She realized her effort to save her children may have endangered their lives instead. Mother took a big breath, swallowing her tears and pain. She sat quietly for a long moment with her head down, thinking to herself.

I cannot let this happen. My children or I can't die. Let me think. Kildong has not returned yet, and Kilyoung has probably put the door on the fort wall by now . . . There is still hope to save them, especially if the children work together.

Once she decided to place her hope in her children together, she felt strong enough to respond to the mayor.

"So be it," she said in a clear voice. "But now that you have interfered with the bet, you will be held accountable for whatever happens after it's completed."

Mother was surprised to feel so much rage in the moment of mortal danger. Maybe it was the unfairness of the mayor threatening her and her children's lives. With the anger came courage she didn't know she had in her. All the patience and wisdom she had gained by raising her unique children, and all the times she felt wronged, became fuel for her. All her life, nothing had been given to her for free. She had never done anything wrong, spending her life trying to survive and protect her children. She wanted to scream at the mayor. *You dare think you can touch even a strand of my children's hair?*

But even in a dire situation, with only the hope that her children would come to rescue her, she no longer felt afraid. She believed in her children. She knew there was love between them, even with all their rivalry and fighting.

"Look how disrespectful you are," the mayor said. "You insult my authority believing your children's strength can protect you. You should be executed on the spot, but I will watch you suffer first.

"Cut Kildong's head off as soon as he returns to the village," the mayor ordered with arrogance. "If he resists, his mother will die instead."

Though terrified of facing Kildong, the soldiers followed the order and went out to arrest him.

In the meantime, Kilyoung heard what was happening and was trying to figure out how to save her mother. All her life, it had never occurred to her that she would be in a position to protect her mother, and she felt frozen with fear.

"Shouldn't you go confront the mayor, Kilyoung? Why aren't you doing anything?"

The townsfolk kept pressuring her. They were concerned that their evil mayor not only squeezed them for taxes but now tried to take innocent people's lives.

Kilyoung looked at the wood plank she would use as the final door on the fort wall. "Here, I am about to win this bet. If I don't finish, I will lose and have to leave the town, never seeing Mother again," Kilyoung said. "Now the mayor says he will kill whoever loses the bet. What do I do?"

"What is there to think about?" one of the townsfolk spoke, frustrated. Shouldn't you get your mother to safety first? You can always make another bet. How is this something to think through?"

"How could I save Mother? As soon as I go to her, I will lose the bet, and the mayor will kill me. I can't just leave everything now. I need to complete my bet first."

Kilyoung's thoughts did not waver far from the bet. The towns-folk could no longer argue with her. They were not sure what to do either. It would not be easy to enter prison and get her mother out. Unless the whole town agreed to fight against the mayor, this act could jeopardize everyone.

"Alright. We will let you decide," the villagers finally agreed. "We will also let you deal with the bet on your own. We do not know if Kildong will return or not."

Still, the people could not help but plead their case once more. "Please, Kilyoung, please stop the mayor." They lowered their heads and begged her once more. "Please stop the mayor and save your mother."

Kilyoung realized that she was faced with an inescapable fate. But she felt immense sadness that when faced with such danger, everyone else could only see how powerful she was.

"Kildong will come back," Kilyoung said, addressing the crowd. "The Kildong I know will come back. The mayor is trying to kill us both, using the bet as an excuse. I am going to win this bet and persuade Kildong to help me. Together, Kildong and I will save our mother. Please wait; you will hear from us soon."

As she finished talking, she completed installing the door into the wall. It was the sturdiest door that she had ever built. The townsfolk all went home, shocked at how Kilyoung chose to finish the door first instead of rushing to save her mother.

As Kilyoung finished the door, she could hear the stomping sound of Kildong's return. She was so happy he was back. But then she paused, thinking how Kildong would destroy everything she built. She locked the door of the fort wall, preventing him from entering the village.

The stomping sound stopped in front of the door.

"*Noona*, it's me, Kildong. I'm back," her brother spoke from outside the door. "I knew you'd finish your task beautifully. I knew it. I knew that you would have already finished it by now."

"Why did you take so long?" Kilyoung shakily asked through the door.

"I learned how useless my strength was on such a mission," Kildong explained. "The iron shoes made my feet bleed, so I could no longer walk. I learned that unless I take care of myself diligently every day, my strength doesn't help me."

"I had been jealous that you got to travel to Seoul," Kilyoung admitted. "I have always been curious about what the outside world is like, but I've never been able to leave the town. The tall tower I built in the middle of the field was so I could see what the outside world looks like."

"The outside world is interesting...," Kildong said. "But full of danger. One has to be on high alert all the time. The journey really exhausted me. I also met several Strongchildren, just like you and me, but they had been chased away from their own hometowns. Apparently, more people are afraid of people like us than those who admire us. They lived as nomads, fighting with random gangs, joining the army, or working as merchants. Maybe that's how to survive in the outside world. I don't know how I should live. What should I do, Kilyoung? I never considered how I would live if I left our hometown."

Hearing her brother speak with such sincerity and vulnerability for the first time, Kilyoung felt heartbroken. She had also never thought about how she would live if she had to leave town. She used to feel frightened and displeased with how unruly Kildong was, but seeing him this honest relieved her. After all, Kildong was just a young man, lost in life, trying to figure out his next steps.

"Kildong, I am about to tell you something important," Kilyoung said. "Something we had ignored before because of our fights and rivalry."

Kildong sensed his sister was about to tell him something that could impact how they would live from then on. "Kilyoung, I know that you won this bet. You can tell me anything, and I will follow," Kildong said. "As long as I can say my goodbyes to Mother before I leave, I am happy to do whatever you command."

"We have not thought about the world outside of you and me. We were so confident that we could do anything we wanted with our strength," Kilyoung began. "We never once doubted that. Maybe we were naïve, but maybe we were just stupid. Perhaps both. That's what I have learned through this bet. Our strength could threaten the world, but that threat also applies to us. The townsfolk were afraid of us. They were just being kind and not letting it show, but they were always afraid and uncomfortable, and somehow we did not notice."

"You are right," Kildong admitted. "We thought people liked us because they let us do whatever we wanted. Whenever I asked them what they thought about something you had made and if I should destroy it, everyone nodded without saying anything, so I believed that that's what they really thought."

"Exactly. That's where we were mistaken. If we were that uncomfortable to the townsfolk, we should have known we were even more of a problem for the mayor."

As soon as Kildong heard the word "mayor" from Kilyoung, he felt his heart drop. He sensed something must have happened.

"The mayor? What did he do?" Kildong asked. "Is it Mother? Is she in danger?"

"The mayor arrested Mother. He told her that whoever loses our bet will be killed. If the loser doesn't obey, he will execute Mother instead," Kilyoung explained. "Soon, the soldiers will be here to kill you. If I don't open this door and you run away, then the mayor may kill me and Mother both."

Kilyoung wanted to see if Kildong had indeed changed his ways and would now actually trust her words. Kildong immediately regretted returning. Here he was, surviving one of the worst pains he had ever known, but all that greeted him was the big sturdy door his sister had built and the threat against his mother's life if he didn't die himself. This was way too much for him to handle. He plopped down and started sobbing loudly.

"No! What do I do, Kilyoung? I do not want to die! I don't want you or Mother to die! What should I do? What should I do?"

Gone were the days of his confident, arrogant self. Kildong wailed like a little boy. Kilyoung could feel just how genuine

Kildong was in his sorrow, and it reminded her of when Kildong was young, he would fall down and cry loudly. Kilyoung's eyes welled up, but her mouth turned into a smile. She realized Kildong was just a boy who wanted to live and still deeply loved his mother and sister.

"I think that you and I, for the first time, should combine our powers," Kilyoung said then. "I know we have not done this before, but one thing is for certain: we must save our mother. Without her, we both know we will be viewed as monsters in this town."

Kildong felt comforted by Kilyoung's voice through the door. He stopped crying, stood up determinedly, and responded confidently, "You are so right, Kilyoung. Let's combine our powers together and save our mother. Let's save Mother first."

Then the siblings whispered their plan through the door.

* * *

The soldiers ordered to kill Kildong had heard his loud iron shoes and knew he had arrived outside the fort. They had expected Kilyoung to open the door for them, but she was nowhere to be seen. No one dared try opening the door, knowing Kildong would be at the other side of the door and that they would not be able to defeat him. They had grown up next to Kildong and knew just how strong he was and, in some sense, admired his strength.

Then Kildong yelled from the other side, "Why aren't you opening this door? My sister built this door so strong I cannot break it. You should open this door for me."

"Kildong, we are not going to open this door because we were ordered to kill you on sight," replied a soldier who had been one of Kildong's friends. "We will just tell the mayor you never returned."

"Kill me? You? Ha!" Kildong let out a roaring laugh. Kildong and the soldiers knew well that a group of meek boys and young men could not hurt him. The soldiers felt frozen with fear. Then Kildong yelled again, "The only people who can kill me are my sister or mother. Nobody else."

Kildong kicked the sturdy door with his iron shoes. The sound vibrated throughout the town as if there was an earthquake. Already terrified, the soldiers started retreating from the door. One of them cried out to Kildong, "But you lost the bet. I thought you were supposed to leave town. Why are you here and threatening us? You can just leave."

"That's right, I lost the bet," Kildong replied. "I would have left town peacefully, but why is my mother arrested, and you soldiers here to kill me? I must get to the bottom of this. Open this door." Kildong continued kicking the door harder, creating loud sounds that shook the whole village.

At the same time Kildong was keeping the soldiers terrified at the door, Kilyoung rushed in the opposite direction toward their mother. While Kildong's ruckus kept the soldiers' attention at the fort door, she would find a way to rescue Mother. She hurried to the prison. As she rounded the hill next to the mayor's station, she saw her mother kneeling before the mayor in the judging courtyard like a criminal.

Seeing her mother still calm and fierce even in adversity, Kilyoung could feel her power rising from within. She looked around and saw a willow tree. She pulled it out from the root and jumped to the middle of the courtyard, swinging it left and right. The force of the wind caused by the swinging tree knocked the mayor, his secretary, and the guards off their feet. Only a few guards were left after the rest had gone away to get Kildong, and those who remained were not prepared to defend themselves. The mayor, disoriented and trying to save his skin, held on to whatever he could to steady himself, but alas, he found himself clinging to the branches of the willow tree Kilyoung was swinging! The mayor was thrown about, dangling from his grasp on the branch.

"How is the greatest mayor hanging on for life at a mere girl twirling some branches?" Kilyoung mocked loudly.

The mayor had never felt more humiliated. "You disrespectful wench! Stop this at once!" he yelled loudly, wanting to keep whatever little authority and pride he had left.

"Why? Does this willow tree belong to you? Or does the wind it's creating belong to you?"

"You dare think there will be no consequences after doing this to me?" the mayor threatened.

"You dare think there will be no consequences after arresting an innocent woman and threatening to kill her child?" Kilyoung countered.

Kilyoung could feel her eyes burning with uncontrollable anger. Her arms pulsed with power as she swung the willow tree. The mayor felt he could faint but was afraid to let go of the branch and be thrown far away. He desperately looked around for help, and all he saw was the pathetic sight of his few men being thrown left and right by the willow tree that Kilyoung was swinging. He could not believe the state that he was in.

With all his might, he told Kilyoung, "Alright, I will consider your love toward your mother. If you stop now, I will spare your life. So stop right this moment."

Kilyoung laughed. "Ha! Only if you swear to leave this town and never return would I spare your life."

"Then who is supposed to rule this town? The King won't allow this."

"Then let the King come kill me," Kilyoung said. "If I am to die anyway, I might as well kill the man who threatened my family first."

The mayor couldn't think of anything else to say. "I will swear your safety!" he finally shouted.

"Hahaha!" Kilyoung felt disgusted at how pathetic the mayor was. But she also wanted to hear something more concrete.

She put the willow tree down in the middle of the prison yard. As she did, the mayor fell on his buttocks and rolled over, unable to even sit or stand. He couldn't do anything but lie on the ground and look at the sky.

Kilyoung looked down at the mayor and asked again, "You? *You* would keep us safe laying around helpless?"

Kilyoung laughed at the mayor. The mayor was humiliated at how Kilyoung looked down on him on the ground. He could no longer know for sure if it was the sky or Kilyoung's face that he was looking up at. Or maybe he was looking at one of the gods. He started sobbing desperately. He had to protect himself from this awful humiliation that was more unbearable than death itself.

"What … is … it … that … you … want?" he finally said. "I … will … let … you … do … anything."

"Leave. Now," responded Kilyoung.

"Then who will rule over this town?" The mayor started crying.

"You never really ruled this town anyway. When have you really ruled over this town? All you did was gather taxes and enjoy the riches for yourself. So leave now and never come back."

The mayor couldn't find any words to respond.

"Go, now, while I give you the grace to save your face," Kilyoung said. "Leave with honor."

The mayor felt defeated. Having experienced this much humiliation for the first time in his life, part of him did want to consider revenge. But Kilyoung's mother, who had witnessed all that happened with such pride, spoke.

"Kildong is protecting the village from the outside. Kilyoung and I will take care of the village," she said.

"Then where am I supposed to go, and how am I supposed to live?" cried the mayor.

"When did you ever care about where or how the townsfolk live?" Mother answered, her voice full of rage. "Go, as long as it's far away. If you leave quietly, you might be able to save your life after all."

The mayor had to choose: either beg them to let him stay even if it meant he would drown in the sea of humiliation or quietly leave while saving his face. He chose to leave right away and ran.

Kilyoung tidied up the debris in the judging courtyard and headed straight to the fort with her mother. Indeed her door held sturdy as Kildong kicked it with his iron shoes. As they approached the door, the soldiers made way for Mother to reach it.

"Kildong, Mother is here," she said.

Upon hearing his mother's voice, Kildong stopped kicking and stomping. All the soldiers hid behind Mother, utterly relieved.

"Mother, are you alright?" Kildong could barely speak, full of emotions. Mother affectionally touched the door as if she were touching Kildong and spoke sadly.

"My dear Kildong, I am so relieved that you are okay. Thanks to you listening to Kilyoung, we were able to get rid of the mayor. He will never come back."

"I am so relieved, Mother! Please open the door now. I returned knowing I lost the bet just so I could see you one last time."

"My dear Kildong, I know, I know. But even so, I cannot open this door. I am so sorry."

Kildong's eyes welled up. "But, Mother . . . !"

"For at least a little while, live outside of town. Stay there until your sister fully forgives you and wants to live with you in town. I will visit you from time to time. Just let me know where you are staying."

"But Mother, I want to see you. Please, let me just see you once," Kildong pleaded.

Mother could feel her heart shattering, but she had to remain strong. She couldn't let go of the peace and safety within such close reach, especially after all that had happened. This was a decision that she had made ten days ago, and it was a decision that would benefit everybody.

"When Kilyoung opens this door for you, I will be the first to see you," their mother said. "That day will come sooner than you think. More importantly, there is an actual reason why you should stay there. This is not a command but my request and perhaps your life's purpose."

"And what could that possibly be, Mother?" Kildong asked.

"The mayor promised to leave town, but neither Kilyoung nor I can trust his words," their mother explained. "The only person that we trust is you, Kildong. If you can, please protect us from the mayor. If it ever becomes too burdensome for you to handle on your own, Kilyoung and I will help. Actually, the whole town will help you. I will see to it that we are here for you. You can trust me, right?"

Kildong nodded quietly as he wiped his tears. He understood what this all meant and responded willingly, "Yes, Mother. I trust you both and will wait until I am called."

"Thank you."

Just like that, Kildong stomped around the perimeter of the town in his iron shoes, outside the fort that Kilyoung made. The mayor ran far, far away until he could no longer hear the stomping sounds.

A few days later, Kilyoung opened the door to leave town herself. She felt that there was nothing else left for her to do there. She couldn't wait to experience the greater world. Kildong met her outside the door and presented Kilyoung with his iron shoes.

"I know you can make even these shoes bigger, better, and more comfortable!" he said.

Kilyoung hung the pair of Kildong's iron shoes on her bag. Their sturdiness made her feel supported. She was unsure what she was about to experience outside of the only town she had known, but seeing Kildong's bright smile and his pair of iron shoes made her more confident than ever. She felt that she would never be afraid of anything now. More importantly, she knew she could always return to her home and family if she wanted.

Kilyoung left on her journey full of confidence. Mother blessed her journey and cheered for her with the townsfolk. It was decided that Mother would rule the town until Kilyoung returned. No one in the village was against this idea because they knew that Mother would communicate well and lead with everyone's best interest at heart, not forcing any commands.

All the townsfolk eagerly looked forward to the day Kildong and Kilyoung would live together in the town ruled by their mother.

About Sunyoung Cho-Park

Sunyoung Cho-Park worked for the feminist magazine IF from 2000 to 2004 and was the content development team leader of Womennet, an organization for women and families. She wrote the feminist play Hysteria before taking a career pause. Park established the feminist book publisher Ifbooks and became the press's publisher and managing editor. She currently hosts the feminist podcast Let's Laugh, Play, and Change the World. She is a feminist content creator who believes that warm solidarity with other women will change the world.

the Story of the Feminist who Rewrote the Story

The famous folktale hero Hong Kildong had a sister.

As a child, I was fascinated with folklore. I listened to the audio folklore series and read all the books I could get my hands on. Rather than the popular Western stories of Cinderella and Snow White, I preferred reading sometimes-scary Korean traditional folktales while hiding under my covers. There were stories about a mean tiger that would spare people's lives only in exchange for their rice cake treats or the brutal, almost-horror tale of the sisters Janghwa & Hongryeon, which was more terrifying than any horror TV show or movie. Because these stories usually had so many unexpected twists and outcomes, I found the Korean folktales fascinating. Perhaps it was not a coincidence that I got the opportunity in my thirties to research and collect different traditional folktales across Korea.

That's when I first discovered many versions of the Hong Kildong folktale across the country. The most well-known, "The Legend of Hong Kildong," written by Huh Kyun from the Joseon dynasty and taught in schools in Korean literature class, was based on a past hero who fought against injustice. However, most of the other versions of Hong Kildong's stories were based on a different myth, a myth of the "Strongchild" who was so physically strong that he changed various landscapes like mountains, fields, and boulders in their region.

The lasting popularity of Hong Kildong continues today, showing up in modern drama, musicals, and theatre, as well as in athletic or household brands. To any Korean, the name Hong Kildong is recognized as heroic and continues to influence many different cultural aspects. This impact seems to have originated from the various evolutions of the original myth of the "Strongchild."

Surprisingly, a version of the Strongchild myth exists that speaks of strong siblings, a boy and a girl. This story is called "Competition between Strong Siblings." In this version, these Strong Siblings lived in a small mountainous village with their widowed mother and entered a very serious bet of physical strength that put their lives at stake. The reason for the competition is not known.

Another example is the myth behind the Mt. Musung Fort near Kongju of Chungnam province. This stone fort surrounding the mountain is now called "Hong Kildong Fort" by the locals, and it is said to be the byproduct of the siblings' competition. What puzzled me was that the fort is thought to have been built by Kildong's sister, yet her name is nowhere to be found. Why isn't it called by her name, or at least "Kildong's sister"? This unfair naming piqued my feminist curiosity. Why was it that Kildong's sister had built this big, strong, and lasting structure yet could not leave her name behind?

When I dug deeper into the myth, this particular story had such a tragic, unforgettable ending. Let me introduce you to a quick summary of "Competition between Strong Siblings."

In a village lived a pair of Strongchildren, a boy and a girl, with their widowed mother. It was difficult for their mother to raise them alone with little money or help. One night their mother had a strange dream. The Mountain god appeared to her and told her that just like there cannot be two suns in the sky, two Strong Siblings could not coexist. Either they both had to die, or only one could live. The Mountain god then said the mother must choose who should live. When the mother awakened distressed, she was unable to make a choice herself, so she suggested her children make a bet. A bet was wagered that the son must wear heavy iron shoes and make a trip far away to Seoul, returning home on foot, and the daughter must build a stone fort to protect their village. Whoever completed the task first would be the winner and survive. The bet began with the boy leaving on his travels while the girl began building the fort. Days passed, and while the mother received no news or signs of her son's return, she watched her daughter's progress with the fort and became anxious. She worried that her son would lose the bet, so she cooked some hot porridge and invited her daughter to rest and eat. She insisted that she believed her daughter would win even with a break. Coerced, while the daughter ate the porridge, the son arrived home, winning the bet. The daughter, upon realizing that her mother had chosen her brother all along, commits suicide by smashing her own head against the stone fort she built.

This is a summary of the folklore, combining only the main components, based on the encyclopedia and academic articles on various regional tales. While some details of the story differ, the central motif stays the same: the Strong Siblings compete over a bet suggested by their mother, putting their lives on the line, and the daughter dies because the mother sabotaged it. Some versions say the daughter hung herself on top of the fort wall; in others, she is pressed to death by a large boulder. In some, the son's shoes are wooden instead of iron; the son travels with or without an ox. The daughter builds a bridge instead of a fort; in others, the brother and sister wrestle. In some stories, the son learns how the bet was fixed and commits suicide himself, then the mother also kills herself, full of regrets. No matter the variety of details, the outcome is the same. The daughter loses the wager and dies.

In yet another version, given that the focus is the competition between a male and a female, the story is a bet between a widow and her suitor or a husband and wife. Of course, the winner is always the male protagonist in these versions. The only exception I found is the story of Halmi Castle in Mt. Palgangsan, where a grandmother and grandfather compete, and the bet ends with the grandmother's win, yet nobody dies.

The folklore of the Strongchildren has been studied by many due to the various versions, tragic ending, male vs. female theme, and usually tied to a historical or old physical structure. Sometimes they are considered the origin stories of historical male heroes who later led revolts and rebellions against kingdoms and other authorities and failed.

The story of Hong Kildong, originating from the myth of "Competition between Strong Siblings," is unique in that the character continues to be considered a powerful and worthy hero who represents the power of the amassed people against the injustice of the powerful few. This image is still so prominent that a theme park was created with that name. Yet Kildong's sister, who was also strong and wise enough to almost win against this powerful hero, failed at leaving her name behind and being remembered.

I started to wonder what would have happened in the story had the mother not intervened? What would have happened? Who would have won?

Before all that, why did such an evil competition have to come about?

How did two innocent children living with a poor widowed mother end up fighting against one another to death?

Who's this Mountain god? What wisdom or benevolence comes out of creating this tragic situation?

How could the mother be so foolish to intervene in this?

How could she even choose one child over the other to die?

These questions aside, nothing about this bet and the outcome indicates any logic or fairness. In fact, the mother created all this tragedy based on a silly dream—such a foolish and evil mother. So then, in conclusion, the villain is the mother . . .

By the time my thoughts reached this conclusion, I had realized that this is just one of the most typical patriarchal stories: mother as villain, daughter as loser, son as ever-victorious hero. Even if he failed to win fairly, Kildong's name is the one retained by history and remembered.

The female protagonist in many different versions of this story—those with the strength and wisdom to compete fairly against the male protagonist—where are they? Why did they all have to die? Was it necessary for them to die? Even when the story explicitly says how these women had strength and wisdom that could be compared to no one, her—*their*—name(s) are omitted from what they have created.

The more I investigated this folklore, the clearer it became to me that the sister from these stories should survive and go on being a hero. If Kildong was a legendary hero that remains to the present time, then his sister should be, too. The fort she made should not be called by her brother's name but by her own full name. I wanted to make all this possible in this rewritten folktale. I began by giving her a name: Hong Kilyoung. Thus this became *The Legend of Hong Kilyoung*.

CHAPTER 3

The Story of Gumiho, the Nine-Tailed One

written by Joyce Park
English translation by Kayoung Kim

"Look at that Gumiho![14] The firefox! With nine tails!"

The boys sang as they ran towards the bottom of the hill. They had been throwing rocks and grass at Gumiho, the nine-tailed fox who lived in the nearby fox hill. But when she started swinging her broom, all the boys scattered, running to and fro.

That morning, Youngho, Mikyung's neighbor, had promised her some good fun. So Mikyung had been standing at the back of the group, smiling, pretending to throw the grass too. But when Gumiho came running with her broom, as all the boys fled, Mikyung tripped on a rock and fell. The pain from the fall aside, Mikyung was terrified of being caught by Gumiho. She had heard stories about Gumihos who feast on children's livers. Her face white with fear, Mikyung barely managed to pull herself up before she saw the heels of the nine-tailed fox through her worn-out shoes.

There she was, nine-tailed Gumiho, huffing and puffing.

---

14)   Mystical creature in Korean legends and folktales that resembles a fox with nine tails with the magical ability to transform to a beautiful woman, often said to seduce boys and young men to eat their liver or heart. The magical power is said to come from a rainbow-hued stone the fox carries.

"There is no tail! There is no tail!" the fox yelled at the boys' backs.

Mikyung flinched and covered her ears. When the boys' voices could no longer be heard, Gumiho stopped yelling and put down the broom she had been swinging. Then, she turned around. Mikyung sat on the ground, unable to speak, completely frozen, shaking in absolute fear. The moment felt like an eternity.

"Is that Porong?" asked Gumiho, pointing to the headband Mikyung wore. Her eyes welling up with terrified tears, Mikyung quietly nodded her head.

"Look how pretty Porong is!" She reached out and touched the headband. Mikyung was uncomfortable sitting with her head down while Gumiho examined the headband. So with a big gulp of bravery, she asked, "Do . . . do you want this?"

"Really?" Gumiho replied excitedly. Mikyung timidly removed her headband and offered it to the fox, deciding that offering her headband was preferable to her liver. Gumiho took the headband with delight, put it on her head, and began searching for something inside her bear-shaped backpack. She pulled out a little mirror to see herself wearing the headband.

At that moment, something else dropped from the backpack. It was a curious-looking rock with a kaleidoscope of colors. Mikyung picked up the rock and returned it to Gumiho, who was busy looking at herself in the mirror.

"So . . . you dropped this. Here."

Grinning at herself in the mirror, Gumiho reluctantly tore herself away from her reflection to look at Mikyung and the rock in her hand.

"Pretty, huh?"

Mikyung nodded in agreement.

"You take it. Exchange for this headband!"

Mikyung nodded again. Whatever Gumiho wanted to take or give, she would agree. It felt strange, though. Gumiho's excitement over the headband and her eyes offering the colorful rock were sweet—innocent-seeming. After feeling so frightened, a wave of relief washed over Mikyung, and her eyes welled up. She noticed her scratched-up knee was bleeding, too.

As Mikyung started to cry, Gumiho began to wring her hands.

"Does it hurt?" she asked. "Do you want me to kiss away the boo-boo?"

Gumiho knelt before Mikyung and started blowing softly on her knee. Looking down at Gumiho's disheveled hair, Mikyung could not decide whether she should stop crying. She caught a glimpse of the colored stone glistening like a rainbow and forgot her tears.

After that, Mikyung carried the rock in her pocket every day. It was prettier than her mother's ring and even more stunning than her sister's hair ribbon. Whenever she held onto the rock in her palm, her heart felt warm and satisfied, like feeling full without eating a grain of rice.

* * *

A few days later, while playing with her friends at school, Jiyoung, a girl so tall that she had to sit at the back of their classroom, asked Mikyung about Gumiho.

"You live near the fox hill, don't you?" she asked. "Does a nine-tailed fox really live there?"

"She lives at the bottom of the fox hill," Mikyung replied. "But she is not a Gumiho after all."

"Oh, but she certainly is one!" Jiyoung rebutted. "Yongsik's uncle saw her. She is the woman with wild hair and a childlike voice who hides in the bushes. Whenever a child walks up the hill, she attacks and eats their liver."

"Whose liver got eaten?" Mikyung asked. Suddenly, Jiyoung felt unsure.

"Well . . . I think I heard it was a kid from the other neighborhood."

"Pffft, you don't even know, do you?" Mikyung challenged.

"Well, the other day, Yongsik and the boys were passing by the fox hill, and they said the Gumiho chased them to eat their livers!"

"She chased them because they were throwing rocks at her. That's why she came swinging her broom!"

"Did you see it yourself?"

"Well, of course, I. . . ." Mikyung began before remembering that she had also been with the group taunting the woman.

"What, did you see or did you not?" Jiyoung pressed.

Mikyung couldn't speak anymore. *I was at the fox hill with those boys throwing rocks at her,* Mikyung thought to herself. *I also ran away when the boys did, but I fell behind. That's how I got to meet the woman called Gumiho, the nine-tailed fox. We spoke and even exchanged our things . . .*

But Mikyung couldn't say all that. At Mikyung's silence,

Jiyoung pointed at her with her index finger and snapped, "See, you don't know."

Mikyung felt frustrated. She wanted to say it was not a scary Gumiho but a nice *unni*, but then she would have to confess the terrible bullying she participated in. So Mikyung kept silent.

That night, Mikyung lay awake next to her older sister Miyoung *unni*, snoring lightly. She couldn't fall asleep. The fox hill seemed so dark from afar, devoid of light. *How does she live there without lights?* Mikyung wondered.

Just then, Mikyung's mom came to check on them, saw that she was still awake, and asked, "Are you not sleeping, Mikyung?"

"I can't sleep, *umma*."

"Why can't my baby sleep?" Mikyung's mom lovingly asked, tucking the blanket around her.

"Mom, is there such a creature as Gumiho?" Mikyung's question made her mom pause.

"Why do you ask?"

"Well, kids call that *unni* at the fox hill Gumiho, the nine-tailed fox."

Her mom looked at Mikyung for a moment before releasing an almost inaudible sigh. "Don't you worry about something like a nine-tailed fox," she said. "And don't go near the fox hill either. Always take the main road. Do you hear me?"

"Kids were following her around, calling her Gumiho," Mikyung insisted.

"Gumiho isn't real!" her mom exclaimed, suddenly annoyed. "Don't hang out with such kids. Why all this nonsense at bedtime instead of sleeping?"

"I just…" As Mikyung searched for words, her mom pulled her blanket up to her chin and tucked her in.

"Go to sleep. It's almost 10 o'clock."

As her mother left the room, Mikyung heard her mutter under her breath. "We need to move away or something. …"

Mikyung had a dream that night. She was wearing a huge skirt, ballooned all around her as if filled with cotton—especially around her butt. She felt self-conscious about the pouf and kept running her hands on her back, trying to flatten the skirt. She was walking past the school playground towards the main gate and heard someone running from behind. Suddenly, she felt her skirt lift from behind and a voice shout, "Look, fox tails! She is a Gumiho!" All the kids outside the main gate came running towards her. Everyone pointed at Mikyung, shouting, "She's a Gumiho! Look at her tails!"

"No, no, no!" Mikyung screamed, waking herself from sleep. Her sister woke too and complained as she turned her back toward Mikyung, "Hey, stop sleep talking!"

Mikyung was so upset from the dream that she cried herself back to sleep.

The next day after school, Mikyung was walking home along the road that ran around the fox hill. Past the bus station, a bridge arched over the little stream, and the street was lined with a few shops, restaurants, and bars. One was a restaurant called Three Peaks Grammy, in front of which stood a group of kids talking amongst themselves. Curious, Mikyung walked over to the group and stood on her toes to glimpse at the commotion. Just then, Gumiho walked out of Three Peaks Grammy, happily carrying something in her arms. It appeared to be food.

"Gumiho! It's the nine-tailed fox!" the kids called out, curiosity gleaming in their eyes. Had Yongsik and his group been there, they probably would have started singing loudly about the nine-tailed fox, but the boys were nowhere in sight.

What a relief, Mikyung thought, but as she turned the corner, Mikyung saw Yongsik and his group squabbling over a small game machine further down the street. Then Youngho saw Mikyung and asked, "Where are you coming from? What's happening over there?"

Before Mikyung could answer, Jiyoung came past Mikyung and answered, "Gumiho is at Three Peaks Grammy!"

"What? Hey, let's go and check that out!" said Youngho, trying to get the boys to join him.

"I want to finish this round first," answered Yongsik, annoyed, his hands still pressing buttons and maneuvering the joystick. Mikyung turned and quickly ran back to the last place she had seen the nine-tailed fox. As she passed an alley, she found Gumiho still smiling. Mikyung grabbed onto her wrist and pulled her close.

"This way, hurry! The naughty boys are coming!"

Mikyung guided Gumiho *unni* between the pharmacy and the hardware store and finally into the back alley. Behind a bar stood big clay pots, and they hid behind them. From afar, they could hear Yongsik and his group running and shouting, "Hey, where is Gumiho?"

Mikyung continued to hide, still holding onto Gumiho's wrist. She stared at Mikyung in surprise. Her face, now without any smile or tears, felt so unfamiliar that Mikyung just looked back at her.

Viewed closely beneath her disheveled hair, Gumiho's face

appeared barely a few years older than her older sister Miyoung's. A pair of puppy-dog eyes were looking straight at Mikyung.

I've seen such eyes, Mikyung thought suddenly. Okja, her family's white mutt, looked like that on the evenings Mikyung's father came home drunk as she tucked her tail between her legs. On such nights, Mikyung's father would arrive home singing his favorite tune, kick the front door, kick Okja a few times, and then kick the small basin in the courtyard before shouting, "Miyoung! Mikyung! My princesses!" Then he often fell down face first, still wearing his shoes.

Just then, Gumiho giggled. "Look, I have a choco-pie. Do you want it?"

As she searched for it, they heard the bar door open, and a few men walked out.

"Sangchul, isn't the kid who's shouting your nephew?"

Sangchul spat onto the ground and answered, "Yongsik must be taunting the nine-tailed fox again."

At the sound of Sangchul's voice, Gumiho froze, holding her breath.

Another voice laughed and chimed in. "Like uncle like nephew. During the daytime, it's the nephew that plays with her. In the evenings, it's the uncle's turn."

"As if you haven't played with her," the first voice countered.

"I don't do it like you. At least I buy her some snacks and give her hair ribbons. I am gentle with her, unlike you, Sangchul. You always hit her."

"Asshole. Be gentle and then take her or beat her first and then take her. Same difference."

Sangchul's voice grew loud, and the other did not respond. Yongsik's uncle was not much bigger than the others, but he was notorious for being "the fist" and having a violent temper. An uncomfortable moment of silence passed until Sangchul spoke up again.

"Hey, you got a light?"

The click of a lighter rang through the alley. With a cigarette in his mouth, Sangchul asked in a conspiratory low voice, "Do you know why Gumiho has nine tails?"

The others burst into laughter. "Others put tails on her, that's why! Let's see, one, two, three of us gave her tails, so does Gumiho now have three tails?"

The men laughed and responded. "Well, she will need six more to become a fully-fledged nine-tailed fox!"

The laughter and voices faded as the men walked away. "Hmm, as far as I know, she already has about seven...."

Sangchul's loud laughter lagged after the long shadow of the falling sun. Once he and the others disappeared, Gumiho's eyes changed, and she started smiling again.

"Gone they are!"

Mikyung could not understand what Yongsik's uncle said about the fox's tails. Gumiho found the choco-pie among her things and gave it to Mikyung, saying, "Here, for you!"

But instead of receiving the snack, Mikyung asked, "*Unni*, do you have tails? Do you really have them?"

Gumiho continued to giggle and gestured at Mikyung to take the choco-pie.

"Do I have any tails?" said the fox, with one hand on her

buttocks. "No tails!" She tapped her buttocks playfully. Tap, tap. "No tails!" Tap, tap. "No tails!" Tap, tap. She kept giggling, tapping, and denying her tails in a singsong voice. Mikyung sighed and picked up the choco-pie from the ground, where Gumiho had dropped it while tapping her buttocks. She put the chocolate snack back into Gumiho's arms.

"I have these at home. You eat it. And take the roundabout way home so that Yongsik doesn't see you, okay?"

Gumiho happily skipped off to her fox hill in a roundabout way, as if dancing. Mikyung brushed off her clothes, leaned forward to see if anyone was on the road, then headed home as if nothing had happened.

That evening, after finishing her homework, Mikyung sat on the flat bench in the courtyard and played with Okja, issuing commands like "sit!" and "paw!" Suddenly, Okja's ears perked up, and her eyes froze, deepening with darkness. She sensed something Mikyung hadn't. Usually, Mikyung's father's favorite song reached the front gate before him, but tonight there was no song. Mikyung bolted up from the bench, opened the front gate, and yelled into the house, "*Appa* is coming home drunk again!"

Then she ran to the back of the house because she did not want to see her father drunk. As expected, Mikyung soon heard the *bang, bang, bang* sound of him kicking the door to the courtyard, followed by three loud yelps as Okja was kicked. But this time, Mikyung's father did not stop after kicking her once or twice; he continued his kicks, yelling, "This bitch of a dog does not even recognize her owner! Hey, bitch! I took you in as a puppy, you fucking beast!"

"Please, stop! Why would you do that to a dog?" Mikyung's mother ran out to the courtyard, trying to stop him. "Why are you acting like this to a dog? Stop it...."

"This fucking dog—when her owner comes home, she's supposed to wag her tail and act happy. She doesn't even recognize her owner!" Mikyung's father yelled in a slurred voice.

"Shhh, stop yelling for all the neighbors to hear. Whatever happened to you today, that you are taking it out on the dog...."

Before mother had a chance to finish, father began yelling again. "That's how you see me? I am such an asshole that I release my anger on a dog because I am ignored somewhere else?"

Yes! Mikyung responded in her head. She really hated when her father was this way. She remembered her grandmother often saying, "He's a good man, except that he turns vile when drunk." He was sweet to his daughters, always calling them "his princesses," but then he kicked Okja and screamed at their mother, complaining about her cooking or calling her a bad daughter-in-law to his parents. No, Mikyung did not like her father.

Every time he shouted, "Am I the asshole?" Mikyung would answer, *Yes, you are!* as loudly as she could in her mind. Feeling satisfied that she had, at least, reproached him in her head, she quietly giggled. Then, her father's loud voice interrupted her thoughts.

"Miyoung! Mikyung! Where are you?" her father called. "Your father is here, and you don't even come out to greet me? Of course, they will be like this when their own mother isn't proper!"

"Go inside the house! Neighbors can hear you!" their mother shouted, walking towards him. "Why are you calling on the girls now?"

Suddenly Mikyung heard her mother yelling, "Let go!" Glass shattered, followed by her mother's cry of pain. Then Okja's barking rang through the air.

Mikyung ran to the yard, "*Umma!*" From inside the house, Mikyung heard her sister Miyoung calling for their mother also.

As Mikyung approached her parents, she saw broken glass outside the front door and her mother sitting on the ground with blood pouring from her left arm. Her father was standing awkwardly, holding onto her mother. Her mother cautioned Mikyung not to come out.

"Don't come out barefoot! You are going to get hurt," her mother said. "Don't come even with your shoes on. What if a piece of glass got into your shoe? Just go inside and find me a cloth to stop the blood."

Still, Mikyung ran to her, crying.

"I am fine," her mother comforted Mikyung. "Don't cry."

Mikyung didn't realize she was sobbing. Miyoung *unni* found a white cloth and brought it outside. Mikyung wanted to help their mother wrap the wound on the arm, but her mother waved her away. Mikyung took a step back and clutched onto Okja. Okja quietly yelped and licked Mikyung's arm. Father sat on the flat bench with a cigarette in his hand. Mother tied the cloth around her arm, then told Miyoung to get her purse and jackets for herself and Miyoung.

"Miyoung will come with me to the emergency room in the city," Mother explained. "I think this needs stitches. We will ask Byungchul to drive us there in his truck. Mikyung, you stay home. Don't touch the broken glass, okay?"

So Mikyung was left behind with her father. As soon as her mom and sister left the house, he said, "Mikyung, bring me a glass of water. Why am I so thirsty?"

Mikyung felt enraged upon hearing her father. It felt like anger was exploding from inside her belly.

"You get your own water!" she shouted. "You do it! You made *umma* get hurt! What is wrong with you? Why are you this way?"

As Mikyung yelled, she plunged toward her father like a ball of fire. He lifted his hand high in the air, shouting, "This ungrateful girl!" Mikyung automatically put her arm up to cover her head. But her dad couldn't bring himself to hit her. He lowered his arm, then kicked the doghouse where Okja was hiding. *Bang! Bang! Bang!*

Father walked on the shattered glass across the courtyard and into the house. Mikyung stood there listening to Okja yelping inside the doghouse, then ran out through the courtyard door. She could see Byungchul's truck, with her mother and Miyoung inside, driving farther and farther away. Mikyung turned and started running toward the fox hill.

As she ran, tears streamed down her face. She grew so out of breath her lungs hurt. She lost track of how far she was running. At first, Mikyung thought her cries were echoing throughout the hills. But soon, the cries she heard in her mind were followed by cries she could hear with her ears. Suddenly, her curiosity won over her grief, and she stopped in her tracks. Mikyung listened and realized she could hear somebody else sobbing even though she was not crying anymore.

Mikyung quietly walked towards a cluster of bushes where the crying was loudest. She first noticed a worn-out broom lying to one side. Next to the old broom, something that looked like a cloth sack was sobbing loudly. Were it not for the disheveled hair and the Porong headband, she would not have known this was Gumiho, the nine-tailed fox. She would have thought there was a ghost within the sack and maybe run away. But finding Gumiho, and not knowing what to do, she stood quietly with her toes moving inside her shoes, then opened her mouth.

"Umm . . . hey, *unni.*"

Gumiho looked up at Mikyung. At first, she was scared and thought about running away, but then she saw the doll Gumiho held in her hand. It looked exactly like a penguin doll that Mikyung used to play with when she was younger. Gumiho was clutching the doll and crying.

"He gave me this doll," muttered the nine-tailed fox through her cries.

"Who?"

"The mister."

"Then why are you crying?" Mikyung asked.

"He gave me this doll, then told me to lie down and close my eyes. But I didn't want to because it hurt. I kicked him because I didn't want to. He was so strong, but I made a long scratch on his face like this." Gumiho demonstrated how she'd scratched the man's face, from eye to cheek.

"I said no! I don't want to! Then he kicked me and hit me. Here, here, and here!" Gumiho pointed to her bleeding lips and torn clothes.

Mikyung thought of her mother, hurt from being pushed by her father, and how her father tried to hit her too. She wanted to sit next to Gumiho and cry too, but looking at her bloody lips, torn clothes, and disheveled hair, Mikyung felt like she was only making a fuss over little things. She sat beside Gumiho and took a piece of gum from her pocket.

"Do you want some gum?"

The nine-tailed fox stopped crying, wiped her tears with her fist, then smiled. "Yes! Give me!"

When Mikyung gave her a piece of gum, Gumiho unwrapped the wrapper and began chewing loudly.

"You can't swallow gum. The gum shouldn't be swallowed," Mikyung cautioned.

Gumiho happily chewed on the gum as if she had forgotten that she had been sobbing just a minute ago. Mikyung put a piece of gum in her own mouth and started chewing. Her nose ran from all her crying, making the gum taste strange. She ignored it and continued to chew as if she was attacking it.

"Is it yummy?" asked Gumiho, seeing Mikyung chew the gum. For some reason, that made Mikyung laugh. At Mikyung's laughter, the nine-tailed fox lady laughed even louder, her mouth open so wide that you could see the gum inside.

If laughter was a circle, Mikyung thought, *these circles would bubble all the way up to the sky.* Their tornado of laughter must have surprised the darkening night sky as the stars seemed to blink as though trying to see what was happening.

When the lights of Byungchul's returning truck appeared on the road, Mikyung gave all the leftover gum to Gumiho and hurried down the fox hill. Her mother returned with Miyoung, looking pale. Inside, they found their father asleep, snoring, the front door wide open. Okja was the only one that greeted them. Mikyung could hear soft thumping sounds from inside the doghouse, Okja wagging her tail. As if she knew better than to wake up their father, Okja did not bark. She just quietly peered out the door of her doghouse and vigorously wagged her tail.

"We will clean up the broken glass tomorrow," Mother said. "Miyoung, give Okja something to eat, then eat dinner with Mikyung."

Mother walked past their snoring father, entered her bedroom, and closed the door.

"I'm not hungry," said Mikyung as she took off her shoes, entered her room, and lay on her blanket. She still had gum in her mouth, but she didn't want to return to the living room to discard it, so she just swallowed it away. Even after all the evening's commotion, sleep was on the schedule. Having seen her mother, Mikyung felt so relieved that she could probably sleep for a hundred years.

The next day, their mother did not speak to Father. Neither Miyoung nor Mikyung looked at him. They hurried through breakfast, avoided their father, and escaped to school.

At the end of the day, as the sisters arrived home and took off their bags, the phone rang. It was their father calling from the bank to say he had left his name seal stamp at the house and couldn't get a deposit without it. He demanded the stamp be sent.

Mother acknowledged his request before abruptly hanging up. She told Mikyung to take the stamp to her father at the carpenter's shop where he worked. Mikyung did not want to see her father but couldn't say no to her mother, who was asking for help, her whole arm completely bandaged. Mikyung left the house to take the stamp to her father.

The shop where her father worked was at the other end of town. Even though she enjoyed the smell of the sawdust and all the little pieces of wood scattered about the floor, free for playing with, she didn't frequently visit because her father told her the carpenter's shop was not a place for girls.

"A girl has no place at a shop where men do their work," he said. "Especially when I am not here, don't come near the shop. You understand?" Once he put it like that, Mikyung seldom visited the shop. Her mother also agreed with her father, so she had no choice.

The shop was loud with the sound of the electric saw cutting wood. Father was working with three or four other workers, someone holding the wood and others holding the saw. Mikyung stood to the side, waiting for her father to notice her.

"Sir, your daughter is here." One of the employees pointed to Mikyung. After a few moments, her father put down the electric saw and removed his goggles. That's when she saw her father's face, where a long scratch ran from his left eye to his cheek.

Shocked, she forgot for a moment why she was there and stared at his face, her mind returning to Gumiho's tears the night before. Father wiped his face with a hand cloth from his waist and spoke kindly as if he could erase all of last night's violence: kicking the dog, breaking the glass, hurting her mother . . . and more.

"My little princess is here. Did you bring the stamp?"

Mikyung couldn't speak. She nodded, took the stamp from her bag, and gave it to her father. Mr. Yoon chuckled as he moved the cut wood to the other side of the shop.

"Your younger daughter seems quite surprised by the lover's quarrel with your wife. Gosh, the women in your house must be headstrong and high-spirited. Whatever could you have done that made your woman do that to your face?"

The father seemed a bit embarrassed. "What do you know about a lover's quarrel when you are still unmarried?"

Then he looked again at Mikyung. She still could not speak. She knew her mother had not given her father that scratch. As she began to hurry away from her father and return home, he called her.

"Here, Mikyung, take this, and buy yourself a snack on your way home." Father placed several bills into her hands, closing her fingers over them into a fist. Then, he affectionately patted her on the behind. Mikyung froze again, returning her gaze to his scratched face.

"Go along now. Go buy yourself some chocolate bars and ice cream, okay?"

Mikyung did not think to open her fist. Instead, she ran the whole way home, knowing exactly what she was looking for. When she arrived, she opened the door to one of the rooms, where she kept all her childhood toys displayed on the piano.

The penguin doll was missing.

* * *

A few months passed. The summer break came and went. During this time, Miyoung and Mikyung stayed at their aunt's house in Seoul. They had a lovely time riding the elevator in their aunt's brand-new apartment and visiting the mountains, aquariums, and even the swimming pool by the Han River. But before long, summer ended. Three days before the new school semester was to begin, it was time for Mikyung to return home.

On the first night after she returned home, she heard some commotion and yelping out in the courtyard, but she was so deep in sleep that she could not wake herself up.

The next morning, Mikyung noticed something was off. Her mother was preparing breakfast with a swollen face. As Mikyung sat by the table, looking around, Miyoung poured water into her cup and said, "Last night, Okja gave birth to her puppies, but they all died."

Shocked, Mikyung asked loudly, "Why did they all die?"

"I don't know. Two of them were born dead, and the other two seemed to move about but died soon after," her sister answered, looking over at her mother. "But Okja wouldn't let us take away her dead pups."

Mikyung's eyes widened.

"Don't worry about it. Eat up and go to school. *Umma* will take care of Okja," said Mother, putting the soup on the table.

"Aren't you going to eat?" asked Miyoung.

"Later. After I feed Okja some bone broth."

Mother took out frozen beef from the fridge. Mikyung couldn't eat, so she hurried to leave the house with her bag. In the courtyard, Okja was inside her doghouse.

"Okja," Mikyung wanted to call out, but she hesitated and left for the school with slumped shoulders.

When she returned home, Mother said that while Okja was eating the broth, she had taken the dead puppies and buried them somewhere in the back hill. Okja weakly wagged her tail upon seeing Mikyung. Usually, she would jump up and down, wagging her tail. Mikyung sat next to Okja and stroked her for the longest time.

You must be sad that all your babies died, Mikyung thought of saying. But she could not quite say it. Even to a dog that may not understand her words, she could not say something like that. She just stroked Okja. Mikyung looked at Okja's fur moving in the wind and slowly stroked the dog again and again. Okja's sad eyes wandered far while quietly accepting Mikyung's tender strokes.

A few days passed. Mikyung was on her way home from school when she noticed a group gathered on the corner in her neighborhood. A woman's shrieking voice pierced through the crowd.

"You slutty little bitch! How dare you show up with that belly after sleeping around with men all over town! Trying to mess up my precious son's life!"

The adults surrounded two women. The older woman continued to scream, snatching the hair of a younger other woman and pushing her onto the ground.

"He gave me a snack. This. This . . . He also gave me a watch." It was the nine-tailed fox. She pulled out a watch and showed it to the older woman.

"So, you say that's the watch Sangchul gave you? My son with a precious future," the older woman shouted. Mikyung saw that the shouting woman was Yongsik's grandmother. "Are you trying to ruin it with a stupid watch? How dare you say the child you carry is Sangchul's after having been with all the men in town?"

Yongsik's grandmother kept raising her voice higher. No one stepped in to stop her. Suddenly, Gumiho screamed and clutched her belly. Sangchul, Yongsik's uncle, had appeared out of nowhere and kicked her in her stomach.

"What crazy bitch? Who do you think you are messing with?"

As Sangchul was about to kick her again, someone suddenly ran out of the crowd and pushed Sangchul. It was Mikyung's mother.

"You can't kick a pregnant woman like that!" she yelled, emotional.

Then, another voice rang out from beyond the crowd.

"What scoundrels, what do you think you are doing?" everyone heard as Three Peaks Grammy, owner of Three Peaks Grammy's restaurant, approached. She was carrying luggage and dressed as if returning from a visit to the city. She dropped her bags in the street and rushed into the crowd. She embraced Gumiho in her arms. The young woman was breathing hard, clutching her belly.

"Call 911! What if something happens to Myunghee?" Mikyung's mother was shaking as she shouted orders to the crowd.

Myunghee, Mikyung thought. It was her first time hearing Gumiho's real name.

"She doesn't even know that her own husband slept with her," Yongsik's grandmother shouted in Mother's direction. "Acting as if she's the one with higher morals. Who can be sure that baby is Sangchul's when it could very well be her husband's?"

Yongsik's grandmother spat on the ground. Mikyung's mom froze. Another crowd member muttered, "Why else would people call her a Gumiho? She has slept with at least nine men. That's why she has nine tails. She's the nine-tailed fox."

"You scoundrels!" screamed Three Peaks Grammy. She began pointing at each of the men gathered, yelling, "You, you, you, you, and you! You buy her snacks, and you give her dolls! You have all taken advantage of a young, mentally disabled woman. Do you think I do not know? She doesn't know right from wrong as long as someone gives her a treat. What have you done to her? Have you got no shame? Does it matter whose baby she is carrying? How can any of you treat a helpless pregnant person this way?"

"Do you have proof?" Yongsik's grandmother challenged. "Where's the proof? Did you see it? If caring for the baby matters that much to you, why don't you . . ." As she raised her voice higher and higher, one in the crowd suddenly screamed out.

"Blood! There is blood!"

Gumiho's skirt was now red, soaking with blood.

"Bring her inside! And call 911. Tell them to hurry!"

Three Peaks Grammy instructed some bystanders to move the nine-tailed fox to her house, and someone began speaking into a phone. Yongsik's grandmother claimed that she needed calming medicine and disappeared. Others started tearing away until only Mikyung and her mother stood in the bloodstained alley. Mikyung's mother was frozen, staring at the blood. Then she turned as though she didn't even see Mikyung or forgot she was there and went home.

Mikyung did not know where to go. She put one foot ahead of the other and ended up by the little shop where some children were playing minigames. There was a stool where one could rest. Mikyung sat. It felt like there was a tornado in her head. Everything was turning around in the tornado. The Gumiho *unni*, Yongsik's uncle, Yongsik's grandmother, Mikyung's father, Okja, Okja's dead babies, the village people . . .

She didn't know what to do with her shaking hands, so she put them inside her pockets. Her hand touched something hard. When she took it out, she realized it was the multi-colored rock Gumiho had given her. It was the very rock that Mikyung loved so much that she once put it in her pocket and looked at it every day. But that day she had put it into her vest pocket was a while ago, and she had forgotten. Mikyung looked at the colored rock for a long time. She stared at where the red started and expanded to meet the blue and create purple, this rock of rainbows. Outside, it started getting dark. Some time must have passed.

"Myunghee, no! Don't!" It was Three Peaks Grammy's voice.

Gumiho was coming out of the grandmother's house, still wearing the blood-soaked clothing. She was holding something in her hands, and it was dripping blood.

"The nine-tailed fox must have taken out a liver to eat!"

Outside the minigame shop, a kid yelled, and panic broke out among the children. As Mikyung rose to approach Gumiho, the fox started running, still clutching the bundle in her hand, dripping blood. She ran out of the neighborhood, and the next minute, the screech of car brakes was followed by a loud thump.

In the dark, it was difficult to see. There appeared to be a truck in the road and what looked like a sack in front of it. The sound of an ambulance wailed through the night. Later, Mikyung wouldn't remember what happened next—not if she walked home alone, if someone found her and brought her home, or how she ended up in her bed.

But that night, Mikyung had a dream. In the dream, she was at the bottom of a stream. She couldn't move. *My body is frozen like a rock!* she thought. Then she heard a loud commotion. She turned to see all the people from the neighborhood around her. They were her human neighbors, but they were also rocks. Yongsik's grandmother was a rock. Yongsik's uncle was a rock. Mikyung's father was a rock. Mikyung started crying, realizing she herself had turned into a stone because of these rocks.

Suddenly, the distant sky became bright, and a rainbow appeared. Mikyung heard a sound and, turning around, saw Gumiho *unni* standing by the riverbank. She was bleeding with nine tails hanging from her body. One by one, she started cutting off her tails, yelping with pain at each one. By the time she cut off her last tail, the long rainbow had reached her feet. Her body was getting brighter and brighter until she glistened. She hugged a white bunny doll in her arms and turned to step onto the rainbow bridge. The rocks by Mikyung started making sounds. It sounded like neighborhood people whispering, "She is a Gumiho, she is a Gumiho."

For the first time, Mikyung called her by her real name. "Myunghee *unni*!"

Myunghee smiled at Mikyung from ear to ear. "I'll come for the colored rock," she said.

Then she turned around, stepped onto the rainbow bridge, and slowly grew farther and farther away.

About Joyce Park

Joyce Park is an essayist, translator, English educator, and activist/lecturer for gender equality and feminism. She is the author of an essay collection, What Little Red Riding Hood Wanted to Say, *a feminist interpretation of Western fairy tales, and of a poetry essay collection called* My Beloved English Poems. *She is also the translator of Anna Russell's collection* So Here I Am: Speeches by Great Women to Empower and Inspire.

*the Story of the Feminist who
Rewrote the Story*

The Significance of Gumiho's Nine Tails

Every neighborhood has one "crazy lady."
All the so-called "crazy" ladies I saw growing up had disheveled hair, wore flowers in their hair, and walked around swinging an old broom. Whenever the neighborhood kids would make fun of these eccentric women, pointing their fingers, the woman would swing her broom to chase them away while giggling. As a young kid, I didn't know any better and thought these women were to be viewed as amusement, like part of a circus act.

Once I was grown enough to read the novel *The Little Darling* by Moon Yeol Lee, I discovered a different perspective on the women who were ostracized by their communities. In *The Little Darling,* the author reminisces about fond memories of growing up in a small town. But I felt nauseated after reading it.

This novel describes a female protagonist who is mentally and physically disabled, with a weak and failed body, but it is written from a man's perspective. In *The Little Darling,* several young men in town abuse, rape, and violate the female protagonist, but in a nostalgic tone, as though the author were sharing happy and beautiful memories. Perhaps the most shocking scene is when the female protagonist asks the male protagonist for help with an itching in her crotch. He tells her to climb up a hill, remove all her clothing, and open her genitals wide toward the sun. Then he and his buddies hide to watch her and entertain themselves.

How could one human be so brazen to use another human

being as an object of entertainment and humiliation? Whether this occurred in the author's real life or is purely fictional, I could not understand how anyone could write this story with such nostalgia as if to reminisce about something beautiful.

Of course, as I continued to get older, I observed several publicized incidents in which a disabled girl or a woman without a proper guardian was raped by several men in her town over a prolonged period.

I further started questioning the identity of the "Gumiho" while exploring the girls and women who were deemed "witches" throughout history. As I learned more about the witch trials that occurred in western Europe from the 13th century to the 18th century, what surprised me the most was how patriarchal Christianity successfully eradicated women's knowledge and power from indigenous European cultures. The image of a witch that exists today is one of a woman stirring a cauldron full of strange herbs and animal parts. However, this is essentially an image of the Medicine Women who were the keepers of knowledge about herbs and women's reproductive health throughout history.

These powerful women, keepers of shared knowledge about fertility, contraception, and abortifacients, came to be represented by the witch archetype because patriarchal structures desperately wanted them and their wisdom to be eliminated. Before the invention of genetic testing, men suffered from fundamental doubts and fears about not knowing if a baby his wife had delivered was actually his. The Medicine Women and their knowledge and skills were viewed as threats to be eliminated.

Of course, other women were killed as well, as Christian patriarchy spread. Those who were old and unable to bear children—and therefore no longer useful to men—and those with the wealth and economic independence that enabled them to use their own voices were especially targeted.

Women as mirrors: sacred or evil beings.

Concurrent with the witch trials of pre-colonized Europe and colonial North America, another movement was underway to objectify women. As the English word "man" refers to both male and human, during the Renaissance, only men were considered fully human. As men developed philosophies regarding the divine, human females became a mere byproduct of humanity. A human male needed a mirror to reflect on himself to appear whole in front of God. Thus the objectification of women only continued.

Francesco Petrarca, one of Italy's three most influential figures during the Renaissance, wrote a sonnet about his worshipful love for a woman named Laura. Dante Alighieri, another poet from the Renaissance era, sang about his everlasting love of Beatrice, whom he wrote about as if she were a goddess. Not only did they paint these women as mysterious sacred beings who do not even go to the bathroom, but these men had never even spoken to these women, let alone held their hands. This type of ideological mystification can only be harmful, as it limits women themselves. Once women are locked into the image of some superhuman deity or goddess, they only further lose agency over their bodies.

It is the double bind of womanhood: women's bodies are either so dangerous as to require eradication or so perfect as to objectify women beyond their humanity.

This type of mystification and objectification of women is why, for example, men secretly install cameras in women's restrooms for their voyeurism. Apparently, it comforts them to humiliate and take advantage of sacred, unapproachable beings.

As women became increasingly objectified and separated from their inherent humanity, another entity was severed from the human experience: nature. In the Renaissance period, the common narratives were those of male writers and artists who captured and objectified women in natural environments. Men projected their own ideas and feelings onto women and nature.

One example is that of the English poet William Wordsworth. After witnessing the king's execution during the French Revolution, a bold, twenty-something Wordsworth publishes the *Lyrical Ballads* with poet Samuel Coleridge. In all their work, there is no suggestion of if or how England's regency might be politically eliminated. To many students of literature and art today, the Romanticism is little more than a collection of love poems, and thus this move might seem very strange; however, at the time, it was revolutionary.

During the late medieval period in Europe, belief in the king's divine right was so strongly held that Shakespeare wrote, "the King's hand is that of a doctor." In historical dramas and movies depicting this period, people often asked the king or other royals to put their hand on a sick child—thought to be a curative measure. This wasn't a symbolic request for a blessing but was based on a genuine belief that the king's hand had the divine power to heal. This belief persisted through the 18th century when Charles II had a medal made in the shape of his own hand and sold it to noblemen to replenish the gold reserve of the kingdom. It was a form of coercive sale of a medal believed to have healing powers. This shows how people viewed themselves not as individuals but as a part of a larger group, with the king as not only the leader of the group but also a divine being appointed by God.

The Age of Reason followed. The 17th and 18th century Europe was known as "the age of reason" because "reason" such as science, medical research, and philosophy became prioritized over dogmatic faith or religious superstitions of before. This also marked the beginning of a time when people would gather those deemed "not reasonable" or "not normal" and place them in government-run asylums.

It would be utterly shocking if we were to review now what they had defined as normal versus abnormal. We can find how normality was determined by looking at the dictionaries published in the 18th century and examining what the most impactful figures of that century had said. Take Samuel Johnson, for example. Before the *Oxford English Dictionary* was published in 1921, the *Dictionary of the English Language* was viewed as the canon and could be found in every household. Samuel Johnson is the genius who singlehandedly created this dictionary after seven years. In this dictionary, words that refer to individual emotional states, such as "melancholy" viewed as abnormal and negative, referring to a person separated from the larger group. Regarding "solitude," Johnson stressed only the physical separation, but in his other works, he warned about solitude, viewing it as a potential pathway to melancholy and other mental health issues.

In this context, Wordsworth published the *Lyrical Ballads,* including poems such as the "Solitary Reaper," which describes a woman who is reaping by herself in nature. In this poem, the poet not only objectifies both nature and the woman gender but also projects all his emotions to her such as loneliness, sentimental, beautiful, and pained. Thus, the woman, along with nature, became the object upon which the male author projected such individual feelings.

The trope of the femme fatale was introduced later in the Romanticism era. In "La Belle Dame Sans Merci," John Keats writes about a woman who suddenly appears from nature and destroys men with her attractiveness. The woman is painted as a mystical, irrational presence who cannot be understood or controlled, just like nature—thus, the two combine in their representation. This precise image is the one that is used to describe the nine-tailed fox (Gumiho) in Korea and China. One cannot help but wonder just how evil and dangerous a fox can be, that this animal is described with a female persona and left so many traces in various folklore.

"She must have seduced him." "She should not have worn those clothes."

Living in the 21st century, when even little children know there is no such thing as Gumiho, we hear statements like those above. Often, when a woman is raped or attacked, the perpetrator or bystanders place responsibility on the woman, arguing that she seduced him or was trying to ruin his reputation and life.

I started approaching the story of the nine-tailed fox in a different light when my thoughts led me to consider that maybe, in the days when many people believed that the tigers smoked cigars and Gumihos existed, a raped woman, unable to speak up, just like the other animals of nature, could be depicted as the mystical and evil nine-tailed fox. Society always has members who are vulnerable and unprotected, whether because of disability, poverty, disenfranchisement, marginalization, or lack of responsible caregivers, especially women. It is not rare to hear stories of these individuals becoming victims of rape or abuse. Not only did this happen in the past, it continues now.

The female monsters in folklore tend to be those who triggered fear in men of patriarchal society or those whom the men had hurt themselves. It is like how leprosy patients, bullied as a fragile minority at one point, suddenly became monsters that ate children's livers in folklore.

There is no nine-tailed fox, only nine rapists.

Today, we see other female monsters who have appeared: Kotbam (Flower Snake), Kimchinyu (Kimchi girl), and Dwenjangnyu (Miso paste girl). The shared characteristics of these women include being seductive and manipulative. These qualities are blamed for destroying men and their wealth—modern folklore for 20th-century capitalism. Women like Daisy Buchanan in the novel *The Great Gatsby* are now the new evil female monsters in modern Korea, where rapid industrialization and globalization have occurred.

Today in Korea, there coexist the Kimchinyu and the Gumiho. Women who are vocal about protecting themselves are criticized via monikers like Kotbam and Kimchinyu, and those that are too vulnerable to defend themselves are condemned under the name of Gumiho.

I share the story of Gumiho now to reconsider the outdated language and myth used to persecute the most vulnerable, those too vulnerable for their voices to be heard. There is no Gumiho—only marginalized, silenced women and girls accused of being Gumiho. I tell this story to highlight a glaring fact: there is no male Gumiho in the old myths. I write this story to call on everyone to unite in solidarity to eradicate this hurtful name-calling and the egregious crimes that precede it.

CHAPTER 4

Heavenly Court Drama: Sun-Nyeo and Woodcutter— Shedding the Pain and Wearing the Heavenly Winged Robe

written by Youngmi Baek-Youn
English translation by Kayoung Kim

Main Characters

Maya: The eldest daughter of Sulhwa (*the Heavenly Maiden, Snowflower*), 14 years of age

Sulhwa: The Heavenly Maiden Snowflower (*Sun-Nyeo*) who retrieved her winged robe

Woodcutter: Maya's father

Woodcutter's Mother: Maya's grandmother

Deer (a buck)

Jade Emperor[15]

Court Secretary

Heavenly Maiden 1

Heavenly Maiden 2

Maya's Inner Voices

Inner-Patriarch   Inner-Antagonist

Inner-Pig

---

15)   Also called *Okhwang Sangje*, Celestial God, is the highest of all gods and goddesses in Korean mythology, responsible for ruling over the humans, gods, and mystical creatures alike.

Act One

SCENE 1

Maya Runs Through the Forest

The DEER—an antlered buck—runs through the woods as MAYA chases after him, dressed in men's clothing. It is a fast and furious chase. The sound of an ax can be heard from afar. The DEER manages to lose MAYA'S chase, follows the sound of the ax, and runs towards the WOODCUTTER. The DEER hides behind the WOODCUTTER'S sling, loaded with logs, and exchanges quick, practiced glances with the WOODCUTTER. MAYA enters the scene running, holding a bow in one hand.

WOODCUTTER
(Nonchalantly.)
Are you chasing a deer?

MAYA nods, too out of breath to respond.

WOODCUTTER
(Points in the opposite direction.)
I saw the deer taking off in that direction.

MAYA

Thank you.

MAYA recognizes the WOODCUTTER'S face. Surprised, MAYA turns away quickly.

WOODCUTTER

Wait! Are you a girl?

MAYA

(Pauses.)

I am a hunter.

WOODCUTTER

You look familiar. Where have I seen . . . ?

MAYA

(Silent.)

WOODCUTTER

Never mind, be on your way.

MAYA runs in the direction the WOODCUTTER pointed. The WOODCUTTER follows MAYA with his eyes as the DEER slowly emerges from his hiding place.

DEER

Goodness, I must be getting old. Of all people
who dare to chase me, a girl!?

The DEER spits loudly and touches his antlers.

DEER (CONT'D)
(Sarcastically to the WOODCUTTER.)
Oh, my pride! Brother, it must be nice living in a
world of total chaos, no structure; it's a mess.

WOODCUTTER
(Still looking in MAYA'S direction.)
The eyes, the mouth, and even the backside look
the same . . .

DEER

The same as who? Oh, that girl there, was that
Sunnam? Wow, she does look just like her mother!
Strange, shouldn't she be up in the sky? What is
she doing running around on the Earth?

WOODCUTTER

She's so grown up.

The WOODCUTTER puts the log sling on his back.

DEER

Like mother like daughter. What a cold-
blooded pair!
(*Shudders.*)
She runs faster than the boys and is better with
a bow. Had I been one step slower, I would
not be alive.

WOODCUTTER

I'm going down the mountain for a drink.

The WOODCUTTER steps heavily.

DEER

Stopping for a drink? Don't you want to go home
to the warm bosom of your new wife?
(*Speaks toward the WOODCUTTER,
walking away.*)
Hey, don't trust your new wife so much. She may
run away, too!

The DEER snickers, exits.

The scene transforms into a dark forest. MAYA enters under the
pale moonlight, carrying a bloody bag.

MAYA

(To the audience.)

They named me Sunnam,[16] hoping they would
have a son next. It worked. My mother gave birth
to twin boys after me.

*(Speaking as if the WOODCUTTER is
standing next to her.)*

Now it's Maya, not Sunnam, Father. Everyone up
above calls me Maya now.

The sound of an owl breaks the silence of the forest.

MAYA

(Responds to the owl.)

Did I miss my father? You want to know, too?
Everyone keeps asking.

With a bitter smile, MAYA pulls out an antler from the bag and
stares at it for a while.

MAYA (CONT'D)

*(Trying to sound cheerful, MAYA speaks
loudly toward the sky.)*

Mother, look! I found something good. I will be
back soon.

---

16)   "Pre-boy."

Act Two

SCENE 1

The Suit & Countersuit in the Heavenly Court

When the lights come on, the JADE EMPEROR stretches, holding onto his throne for balance, while his COURT SECRETARY pulls lawsuit paperwork from the clouds.

JADE EMPEROR

How many more do we have left for today?

COURT SECRETARY

This is the last one of the day.

JADE EMPEROR

I am exhausted. What is this lawsuit?

COURT SECRETARY

Your Highness, this is a suit and countersuit between an animal and a human.

JADE EMPEROR

This is becoming a fad now. Wasn't there a similar
one between a rabbit and Yong Wang?[17]

COURT SECRETARY

Oh yes, the case with the liver. The rabbit
won that one.

JADE EMPEROR

Let's see . . .

The JADE EMPEROR sits on the throne and looks at the docu-
ment handed to him.

JADE EMPEROR (CONT'D)

This is a long list! One side is accused of coercion
to marry, abduction, imprisonment, destruction
of property, sexual and domestic violence . . .

COURT SECRETARY

And the other side is being countersued for habit-
ual violence and bodily injury.

JADE EMPEROR

I am already tired from hearing this.

17)   God of water, also translated in some texts as Dragon King.

COURT SECRETARY
(Calls in the accused.)
Will the accused enter!

The DEER and MAYA enter. The DEER has his head wrapped up in a bandage, and MAYA has a bow on her back. Both kneel in front of the throne. The DEER huffs and puffs as if frustrated, and MAYA appears calm.

COURT SECRETARY
Who wants to speak first?

DEER
Jade Emperor, I am so incredibly frustrated and upset. Look here. I have blood coming out of my head like a waterfall. That girl attacks me like a crazy person whenever she sees me. I have done nothing wrong; I am the victim. I am just an innocent animal that eats grass and chases butterflies.

JADE EMPEROR
(To Maya.)
Do you accept these charges?

MAYA
I did cut just a little bit of his antlers.

DEER

For us males, our antlers are our life. Looking like
this, I can't even find a mate. If my family line
stops because of you, will you take responsibility?
You should have just cut my head off instead!

MAYA flashes a cold smile and threateningly gestures as though
to slice the DEER'S throat.

DEER

See? You're threatening me. We have
witnesses here.
 (Gestures to the audience.)
You saw her threatening me, right? Right?

COURT SECRETARY

Silence!

JADE EMPEROR

What did you do with the cut antlers?

MAYA

My mother is very sick, so I used them as
a medicine.

DEER

(Sarcastic.)

My, what a good daughter. Do you want a prize instead of a lawsuit?

MAYA

What is the harm of being a good daughter who cares for the mother who birthed and raised me? Is it strange?

DEER

Yeah, it is very strange that you express your gratitude using my body. Is that how your *Sun-Nyeo* mother taught you to behave?

MAYA

(Infuriated.)

Don't drag my mother into this if you don't want me to cut off something else.

DEER

(Looks down at his crotch.)

Wha . . . What?

MAYA

I mean your *tongue*. If you hadn't used that tongue . . .

COURT SECRETARY

Be quiet, both of you. How dare you make such a
fuss in front of the Jade Emperor.

JADE EMPEROR
(To the COURT SECRETARY.)
Her mother is a Heavenly Maiden?

COURT SECRETARY

Yes, you remember the one? She went down to
Earth to bathe a few years ago and gone missing.
Everyone thought she was killed by some wild
animals, but one day she returned unharmed.

JADE EMPEROR

Yes! The youngest one . . . Her name was . . .
Sulhwa—Snowflower.

COURT SECRETARY

Yes, this one here is the eldest daughter of Sulhwa.

JADE EMPEROR

Is that so . . .

The JADE EMPEROR points to MAYA.

JADE EMPEROR (CONT'D)
So, she is half-blooded?

COURT SECRETARY

Yes, a halfie. Mixed, multicultural.

DEER

She is evil. Once my wound finally heals and the
antler starts to grow—and I start to feel like a
buck again—she attacks out of nowhere. Again,
chop, chop . . .

The DEER starts sobbing.

JADE EMPEROR
(To MAYA.)

Why did you do such brutal things unfit for a
girl and then sue the deer? As the daughter of a
Heavenly Maiden, your behavior should be more
feminine and modest.

MAYA

Forgive me, but this is not about the deer's antlers.

MAYA arranges her hands politely.

MAYA (CONT'D)

I am making a desperate plea. Please get to the
bottom of this and determine right from wrong,
so the injustice done to my mother can be righted.

JADE EMPEROR

Injustice? There must be a story behind this.
(Sits up straight.)
Alright, let's hear it.

MAYA

This deer did something 17 years ago that has caused my mother, me, and my two siblings to live in pain ever since. This deer talked my father into stealing my mother's winged robe, trapping her on Earth, and forcing her to marry him. As a result . . .
(In a sad and painful tone.)
I was born . . .

DEER

This is nonsense! Do you even hear yourself? Thanks to my kind deed connecting a young man with a Heavenly Maiden, the three of you were born. You should be thanking me for giving you life! I was simply showing my gratitude after the Woodcutter saved me from a hunter's trap.

MAYA

My whole life, I've never had a day of peace. My mother was always sobbing quietly.

MAYA kneels and bows to the JADE EMPEROR.

MAYA (CONT'D)

He is the cause of so much tragedy and pain.
Please send this deer to the heavenly prison or the
fiery hell.

DEER

Your Highness, I feel so wronged. This girl is too
young to know how things unfold between a man
and a woman.
　　(To MAYA.)
Down on Earth, males seduce and mate with
females; they have babies and live together.
Okay, maybe your life was a bit hard growing
up, but you should be talking to your parents
about it instead of shooting your arrows at an
innocent deer.

MAYA

If you wanted to show gratitude to the
Woodcutter, you should have offered him
something that belonged to you. Why did
you give away my mother's entire life as your
compensation?

COURT SECRETARY

Yeah! You could have told the Woodcutter where
the wild ginseng was buried or even given him
your antler.

JADE EMPEROR

(Coughs to get attention. Whispers.)

Hey, hey, neutrality, neutrality.

COURT SECRETARY

(Bows his head.)

Sorry, your highness.

MAYA

Do you know how my mother, I, and my brothers suffered because of you?

(Becomes emotional.)

My mother grieved and cried every day because of you! Do you know what it is like to live with such sadness daily? You are an evil bastard!

DEER

(Infuriated.)

A woman should learn to accept her fate! I didn't know how small-minded your mother was. I'm sorry for not knowing what a mess your mother became. But honey, you wouldn't even be here if not for me. You should bow down to me with gratitude for making your life possible.

MAYA

You're crazy! I am going to kill you for good!

MAYA runs toward the DEER.

The DEER and MAYA get into an angry, physical fight.

The COURT SECRETARY breaks the DEER and MAYA apart with some difficulty.

COURT SECRETARY

How dare you! This is the emperor's courtroom!

JADE EMPEROR

(To himself.)
Well, this is a headache.
(To the COURT SECRETARY.)
I want to know everything that is related to this case. First, bring me this girl's father.

MAYA

Your Highness, if so, please investigate both my father and my grandmother. They are accomplices in this crime.

JADE EMPEROR

What? You not only want your father but your grandmother in the courtroom also?

MAYA

Yes, please hear all sides of the story. Listen to
my mother's testimony and the other Heavenly
Maidens who traveled down to Earth to bathe
with her seventeen years ago.

JADE EMPEROR

Now you want to involve heavenly people in
this, too?

MAYA

Your Highness, I have waited my whole life
for this day for you to deliver justice. Please be
thorough and attentive. You can even ask for
testimony from the townspeople who knew the
entire story and never did anything. They are all
accomplices in this crime.

JADE EMPEROR

I will take care of this.

MAYA

But . . .

MAYA stops herself short.

COURT SECRETARY

Look how disrespectful and demanding you are!

DEER

See, I told you she's crazy!

JADE EMPEROR

(Displeased.)

You are indeed being disrespectful and demanding . . .

COURT SECRETARY

Your Highness, I will punish her for this.
(Turns toward MAYA.)
You!

The JADE EMPEROR stops the COURT SECRETARY.

JADE EMPEROR

(To MAYA.)

I see how desperate and upset you have been through this.

MAYA

(Bows down to the ground.)

Thank you, your Highness.

JADE EMPEROR

My head . . .

The JADE EMPEROR presses his temples for a minute.

JADE EMPEROR (CONT'D)

Alright. I shall question your father and your grandmother first.

COURT SECRETARY

As you command, your Highness.

MAYA

Thank you, your Highness.

Act Three

SCENE 1

Maya's Inner World: "Eat, Forget, and Run"

One chair sits centerstage. The chair represents the seat of MAYA'S SELF—her consciousness. MAYA has a hard time being the owner of the chair. There is a lot of fuss among her various selves: their voices and opinions. MAYA'S INNER VOICES—the INNER-PATRIARCH, the INNER-ANTAGONIST, and the INNER-PIG—all try to grab the chair to have control over MAYA'S SELF. MAYA stands furthest from the chair while INNER-PATRIARCH and INNER-ANTAGONIST fight for the seat.

> INNER-PATRIARCH
> (*Sits on the chair while blaming INNER-ANTAGONIST. With sarcasm.*)
> Good job. Just look at the mess you've created in the courtroom.

> INNER-ANTAGONIST
> (*Holding on to the chair.*)
> Of course, I did a good job. Did you think I would stop my efforts after merely scaring the deer a little?

INNER-PATRIARCH

(Sarcastically.)

You must be pleased now that you've accused both your father and grandmother of being criminals.

INNER-ANTAGONIST

It needed to happen, and if not now, when would we get our justice served?

INNER-PATRIARCH

Even so, there are such things as morality. You've now made Maya out to be an ungrateful, entitled bitch who doesn't respect her elders. Who is going to take her side now?

INNER-ANTAGONIST

I am trying to show who acted immoral in the first place.

INNER-PATRIARCH

Why are you trying to stir up the past? You're only bringing shame and dishonor to the family.

INNER-ANTAGONIST

Feel free to be the only one who worries about other people's thoughts.

INNER-ANTAGONIST pushes INNER-PATRIARCH and sits on the chair instead, making a cold face at MAYA.

> INNER-ANTAGONIST (CONT'D)
> It could have gone better. You finally had a chance to speak the truth, and you could have been clearer, more articulate, and more elaborate in showing all the wrongs they committed. Instead, you just became emotional and started fighting with the deer. This will not benefit us. People will say you are the one with personality problems. Maya, stay sharp. Let's do better, you hear?

With the two INNER-VOICES criticizing her, MAYA feels small and anxious, intimidated by INNER-PATRIARCH, and made inadequate by INNER-ANTAGONIST.

> INNER-PIG
> *(Enters carrying a short table full of food, stepping lightly.)*
> That's enough already.

INNER-PIG easily pushes both INNER-PATRIARCH and INNER-ANTAGONIST out of the way by force since the Pig archetype is very strong.

INNER-PIG smiles warmly at MAYA.

INNER-PIG (CONT'D)

My dear, you poor thing. That must have been
really hard for you, even though you put on a
brave face.

>   *(Pushes a spoon into MAYA'S hand.)*

Go on, eat. The fried fish cake is especially
yummy today.

>   *(Puts a piece of fried fishcake into*
>   *MAYA'S mouth.)*

Now, let's start with the rice, okay?

MAYA looks timidly at INNER-PATRIARCH and
INNER-ANTAGONIST.

INNER-PIG

>   *(Waves food in front of MAYA to get her*
>   *attention.)*

Try this.

>   *(Places food in MAYA'S mouth.)*

Delicious, yes? Picky eaters lose the blessings, too.

INNER-PIG drinks a bowl of rice wine and wipes her mouth.
INNER-PIG offers a bowl to MAYA.

INNER-PIG (CONT'D)

Drink it all. There you go, bottoms up.

MAYA is finally relaxed and starts shoving food into her mouth.

INNER-PIG

Our Maya is the fairest when she eats!
(*In a singsong voice.*)
If we eat well, we will even die well. It's all
about food.

MAYA eats and eats more rapidly and mindlessly. The INNER-
PATRIARCH and INNER-ANTAGONIST approach quietly.

INNER-ANTAGONIST

(*Is shocked and pushes
INNER-PIG away.*)
You ate all of this? All this food?
(*Takes the spoon away from MAYA.*)
We don't have time to waste! We must prepare for
the subsequent trial. There is so much to prepare.
Even if we worked all night, we might not accom-
plish it all.

INNER-PATRIARCH

(*Flips over the table of food angrily.*)
You have the audacity to eat? After bringing such
shame to our family?!

MAYA

(*Gathers the food that has fallen on the
floor with her hands.*)
I eat and eat, and I still feel hungry.

MAYA shoves more food into her face and smiles strangely.

INNER-PATRIARCH

Disgusting! Nobody will ever want to marry
such trash.

INNER-PIG

Yes, baby, I know. It's because your heart
feels empty.
>   *(Puts the spoon back into*
>   *MAYA'S hands.)*
Eat. It's all about food. I will take care of these
annoying ones.

INNER-PIG turns around to stare down INNER-PATRIARCH
and INNER-ANTAGONIST.

Music fitting for a battlefield begins to play. All the INNER-
SELVES start fighting. Finally, INNER-PIG knocks the others
down, defeating them. At that precise moment, MAYA hands
INNER-PIG the empty bowl.

MAYA

More, please.

INNER-PIG
(*Huffs and puffs in a very
affectionate tone.*)
Yes, dear, just wait. I will bring you
another spread.
(*Glares at the others.*)
Don't mind a word these fools say, you hear me?

INNER-PIG picks up the table and leaves.

INNER-ANTAGONIST
(*Shakily gets up, grabs MAYA'S
shoulders, and shakes her.*)
Come to your senses! We don't have time for
this! Maya, leave it to me. I'll take over at the
subsequent trial.

INNER-PATRIARCH
Nobody is going to believe a word that's coming
out of a mere girl's mouth.

INNER-ANTAGONIST
I know it. People should never know you are
like this.
(*Rubs MAYA'S back.*)
Let's get it all out. Get it all out of you, and you
will be clear-headed. Then we can prepare for
the trial.

INNER-ANTAGONIST pats MAYA'S back.

MAYA starts throwing up all the food, suffering.

> ### INNER-PATRIARCH
> I am telling you, women always cause problems
> in this family. They are the troublemakers. Her
> mother takes off all her clothes and acts crazily.
> This one binge eats and pukes.

> ### INNER-ANTAGONIST
> *(Hurriedly covers INNER-*
> *PATRIARCH'S mouth.)*
> Shh, don't mention that about her mother. Let her
> please forget that memory.

INNER-PIG comes back with a table full of food again. INNER-PATRIARCH and INNER-ANTAGONIST slowly back away, intimidated by INNER-PIG.

> ### INNER-PIG
> *(To the audience.)*
> You want to know why she keeps eating? To live!
> To survive! What does she have in her life to look
> forward to, if not the joy of eating?
> *(To MAYA.)*
> Isn't it, my dear? Here, eat, eat more. Eat and forget
> about all the pain. Eat, and you can go to sleep.

MAYA happily reaches toward the new table full of food. Now, the Chair—the seat of MAYA'S SELF—belongs to INNER-PIG for a long while.

Act Four

SCENE 1

Testimony in Heavenly Court: "The Heartbreaking Sound of the Wind"

On one side of the stage stands the WOODCUTTER and the WOODCUTTER'S MOTHER—MAYA'S GRANDMOTHER. On the other side of the set is MAYA. They are all kneeling on the floor in front of the JADE EMPEROR. The JADE EMPEROR unrolls a scroll and reads the content of the lawsuit. The COURT SECRETARY is beside him, assisting.

COURT SECRETARY
(To the WOODCUTTER.)

I remember when you were like a lonely rooster
who would cry day and night. But now you look
like a man again. You look well.

WOODCUTTER

(Bows down.)

It is all thanks to the Jade Emperor.

JADE EMPEROR

I felt moved by how dedicated he was to his old mother. Now I see that he had to part forever with his *Sun-Nyeo* wife. I feel bad for him. As the father of all the Heavenly Maidens, the Woodcutter had been my son-in-law, after all.

COURT SECRETARY

(Sifts through the scroll.)
I see that you have gotten remarried already?

JADE EMPEROR

(Surprised.)
Is that so? Hmm …

WOODCUTTER

It is difficult to move on and forget my *Sun-Nyeo* wife. But my mother is old, and …

GRANDMOTHER

(Interrupting.)
He must carry on his family name. Without that, there will be no one left in our family to perform the ancestral ritual after I die.

JADE EMPEROR

(Nodding.)
I see.

MAYA

I can perform the ancestral ritual for you.

GRANDMOTHER

You will marry someone and become a part of his
family, performing their ancestral ritual. This is
why everyone wants to have sons.

MAYA

You have not changed a bit.

GRANDMOTHER

(Getting angry at MAYA.)

Thanks to you, I am here visiting the heavenly
court even before my death. You are just like your
mother, ungrateful and demanding. Her greed
made all this happen. She is a bad wife who left
her husband, and now this trial embarrasses the
family even more!

WOODCUTTER

Mother, please calm down.

GRANDMOTHER

What, isn't that true?

GRANDMOTHER steps in front of the JADE EMPEROR.

GRANDMOTHER (CONT'D)

(In a desperate voice.)

Your Highness, I won't ask to get the *Sun-Nyeo* daughter-in-law back, but . . .

(Starts sobbing.)

My grandsons! Please allow me to reunite with my grandsons.

(Wipes away her tears.)

When my daughter-in-law was making her fuss in her winged robe, I begged her. I cried and begged her to leave the boys behind. Your Highness, I still pray to you every night, making an offering with a bowl of water, hoping for the return of my grandsons!

COURT SECRETARY

I thought you had long since changed your prayers to wishing for a new grandson from your new daughter-in-law.

GRANDMOTHER

(Sheepishly.)

Well, that is . . .

WOODCUTTER

Mother, please calm down.

(Turns to MAYA.)

Hey, Sunnam.

MAYA

It's Maya.

COURT SECRETARY

She received a new name when she arrived here
seven years ago.

WOODCUTTER

Sunnam, your mother surely knows that I am
here, too?

JADE EMPEROR

Right, why isn't your *Sun-Nyeo* mother
here today?

MAYA

She is too ill to stand this trial, your Highness.

JADE EMPEROR
(*Whispers to himself.*)

I understand nobody has seen her coming out of
the house for years.

MAYA

I have witnessed everything, so I can represent her
on her behalf.

JADE EMPEROR

(Sifts through the scroll.)

Let's see. The crimes of coercion to marry, abduction, imprisonment, destruction of property, sexual and domestic violence . . . These are many serious crimes. Did you indeed commit all these crimes?

GRANDMOTHER

Your Highness, that's nonsense. How could common folks like us do that to a Heavenly Maiden, especially one who is your daughter?

WOODCUTTER

My only crime is that I loved her too much. Your Highness, you should know this!

JADE EMPEROR

Yes, I thought so, too. I imagined the Heavenly Maiden was happily married on Earth but was too homesick and made the difficult decision to return to the heavens. That's why I allowed you in when you once returned, riding a magical wooden bucket. But now, you must explain why your own daughter accuses you of all these crimes.

COURT SECRETARY

Start telling your story truthfully to the divine
Jade Emperor.

JADE EMPEROR

Start with how you were able to marry a Heavenly
Maiden in the first place.

WOODCUTTER

(Stammers.)

I . . . I really only did what the deer told me to do.
The deer told me to steal the *Sun-Nyeo*'s winged
robe from her and hide it, so she couldn't fly away
and return to the heavens. The deer told me never
to return the robe to her unless she gave me four
children. But I am too softhearted. I showed her
that I had taken the winged robe too soon. That
is my fault. Had I not been so stupid to show her
where the winged robe was hidden, she couldn't
have left me.

JADE EMPEROR
(Gives the WOODCUTTER a
piercing look.)

So your mistake was only that you showed her the
winged robe?

WOODCUTTER

I should have followed the deer's instruction to
the very end.

JADE EMPEROR

What made you disregard the instructions after
having hidden her winged robe for eleven years?

WOODCUTTER

That day, Sulhwa wasn't crying or angry like the
other days. She was actually smiling and calling
me her husband. That day she truly looked like a
Heavenly Maiden . . .
    (Catches himself forgetting his audience.)
I finally felt like she was indeed my woman.

GRANDMOTHER

Oh, you stupid boy! You were manipulated by her
begging that she wanted to try on the robe one
last time!
    (To the JADE EMPEROR.)
That's not all. She lied and coaxed my son to show
her the hidden winged robe all these years. She
even told him it would make an excellent gift for
the king, and he would be rewarded for offering
such a gift, and . . .

MAYA

(Interrupting.)

Grandmother, you are the one who used to tell him to sell the winged robe in order to clear his gambling debt!

JADE EMPEROR

Gambling?

WOODCUTTER

(Hurriedly.)

Mother, this is all my fault. Please stop talking and forgive me.

JADE EMPEROR

I want to ask a question. How did Sulhwa act when you first stole her winged robe?

WOODCUTTER

She was lovely.

JADE EMPEROR

(Leads the WOODCUTTER to tell more.)

Oh, lovely, was she? In what way?

WOODCUTTER

She was frantically looking for her robe when I appeared. When I surprised her, she jumped back into the water. She was left alone after the other *Sun-Nyeo*s flew back to the heavens.

JADE EMPEROR

And?

WOODCUTTER

She was so shy, only peeking her head out of the water. No matter what I did, she wouldn't come out of the water all night. She was so cute and sweet. She drove my heart crazy all night.

MAYA

She was terrified, not shy!

COURT SECRETARY

Silence!

JADE EMPEROR

I see. Then what happened?

MAYA

Your Highness, why do you need to ask . . .

JADE EMPEROR

(*Ignores MAYA and speaks to the
WOODCUTTER encouragingly.*)

Go on.

WOODCUTTER

(*Excited by the JADE EMPEROR'S
encouragement.*)

I promised I would treat her well if she married
me. And I told her I would even return her
winged robe if she bore me four children.

JADE EMPEROR

And then what happened?

WOODCUTTER

She was such a tease. She wouldn't come out even
when the sun rose, so I had to jump into the water
myself and pull her out. Then I ran straight home.

GRANDMOTHER

(*Pleased.*)

I thought my son was only kind and docile, but
he was a man, after all. He came home at dawn
carrying a Heavenly Maiden on his back. She
must have been a prize from you for being such a
good man, your Highness.

JADE EMPEROR
(*Puzzled.*)
I gave her to you?

WOODCUTTER & GRANDMOTHER
(*Simultaneously.*)
Yes.

COURT SECRETARY
Show your respect! The Jade Emperor does not get involved in such human business. This was all your own . . .

MAYA
Grandmother immediately set up bedding for them, and then my mother was . . .
(*Pauses.*)
After that, my mother lost all hope. She thought she couldn't return to the heavens with the shame and ruin of what happened.

GRANDMOTHER
As the old saying goes: a woman's life is like a water gourd; depending on who uses it, life could be precious or lowly. At least your father treated your mother preciously, don't you remember?

MAYA

He locked her in the house, saying she was too beautiful for the outside, like a flower. And you were always so unhappy with my mother.

GRANDMOTHER

Now, what are you saying I did?

MAYA

I remember how you treated my mother when my father was not home.
(*Reminiscences.*)
Mother was so good at acupuncture and healing. She was better than famous human healers. Her services were even requested at noblemen's homes, and she returned home with meat and silk in exchange for her treatments.

GRANDMOTHER

I kept telling her she shouldn't be more capable than her husband—that's bad luck for keeping a husband faithful.

WOODCUTTER

(Interrupts, realizing
GRANDMOTHER is speaking
too much.)

You mean, we couldn't let my fragile, beautiful wife go out and work in this difficult, dangerous world?

GRANDMOTHER

(Catches herself.)

Yes, that's right. I raised my son to work hard and take on difficult work outside the home to shelter his wife.

MAYA

(Frustrated.)

Father said women could only make pocket change, but Mother was making more money than he did. Grandmother didn't like that and kept criticizing her, calling her a bitch who stole her husband's energy and abilities.

GRANDMOTHER

A woman should never try to compete and win over a man. That's the natural law on Earth.

JADE EMPEROR
(To MAYA.)
Hmm ... Continue.

MAYA

At least, it was okay before my brothers were born.
Everyone doted on me.

WOODCUTTER

Oh, you do remember!

MAYA

(Eyes well up as she reminisces.)
When I was little, I was always on my father's lap.
His beard scratched me, and I tried to escape,
but he would hold me so tight and not let go. I
can still remember his smell, a mixture of sweat
and alcohol.
(Pauses with sadness.)
But once the twins were born, everything
changed. Grandmother started to treat Mother
and me as maids who only cooked and cleaned.
Mother couldn't even hold her babies after
breastfeeding because Grandmother would take
them away as soon as they were fed. She could
only look at them from afar because Grandmother
kept my brothers in her bedroom as if they were
her babies.

GRANDMOTHER

I was only trying to help my daughter-in-law. She
was always a bit fragile!

MAYA
(To GRANDMOTHER.)

The twins were not her grandchildren; they
were her sons.

GRANDMOTHER

You are an ungrateful child after all the trouble I
endured raising you and your brothers.

JADE EMPEROR
(To GRANDMOTHER.)

Why did you keep the twins away from their
mother? Look into my eyes so you will answer
truthfully.

The JADE EMPEROR begins to use magic to pressure
GRANDMOTHER to tell the truth.

GRANDMOTHER starts shaking her body in pain, then
suddenly relaxes.

GRANDMOTHER
(Has a hazy look on her face.)
A human dared to forcibly take a Heavenly Maiden.
I figured she would eventually abandon my son and
return to the heavens. That's why I had to hold on to
the boys. We need boys to carry on the family name.

MAYA
There were days when Mother would have attacks
of sobbing while sewing and mopping. She would
weep, her face filled with longing, and talk to
herself. Father couldn't deal with her on those
days. Especially if he'd had a lot to drink.

The scene is interrupted by the sound of the wind and a door
shaking in the wind.

HEAVENLY MAIDEN SNOWFLOWER
(Offstage, voice only.)
Please let me go. Please let me live.

MAYA
(Cannot bear the sound.)
Can you hear that?
(Purrs.)
The winds. The sounds of a ripped paper screen on
the window. That night, I saw everything through
the torn window screen, Father. Everything.

JADE EMPEROR

What is it that you saw?

MAYA

Father hit Mother. He kicked her, hit her with his
fists, and threw things at her.

JADE EMPEROR

What? He dared to lay hands on a
Heavenly Maiden?

WOODCUTTER

No, your Highness. How could one from a lowly
life like mine dare do such a thing?
 (To MAYA.)
You saw wrong. You were too young, and your
memory is not accurate. No. I did not do that.

JADE EMPEROR

You shall speak the truth, and only the truth, or I
will throw you in the face of the fire!

WOODCUTTER

 *(Wrings his hands and begins backing
 out of the room.)*
No, I never did such a thing. I feel wronged,
your Highness.

(To MAYA.)
How dare you do this to your own father? Did
your mother brainwash you?

JADE EMPEROR
(Infuriated.)
Truth!

Sound effects begin. As the JADE EMPEROR starts using his
magic on the WOODCUTTER, MAYA, who had been shaking
and scared in the background, starts sobbing.

MAYA
(Eyes are out of focus.)
Mother's clothes were . . . red . . . with her blood . . .
(Starts wailing like a little girl.)
Umma! Umma . . .

WOODCUTTER
Okay, I admit, when *Sun-Nyeo* would refuse me
in bed or not bring me meals promptly when I
requested—when she acted so stiff and cold to me
all the time—all I wanted to do was to put some
sense into her. I only laid hands on her slightly—
just a little bit.

MAYA
(*Out of breath with her flashback.*)
Father broke out of the room and into the
courtyard like a crazy man. He found a sickle
and started walking back into the room where
Umma was! No!

The scene is interrupted by the sound of wind and a window
screen vibrating. The sounds become louder.

The JADE EMPEROR performs magic. The JADE EMPEROR,
the WOODCUTTER, and MAYA are now in the scene inside
MAYA'S memory.

MAYA enters a state of trance and starts speaking as SULHWA.

MAYA & SULHWA
(*Simultaneously.*)
Please, please don't hurt me. Don't kill me.

WOODCUTTER
(*As if holding a sickle in his hand, he
raises his hand to MAYA, who is acting
like SULHWA.*)
Let's just all die. I am going to kill you, myself,
even these damn kids.

GRANDMOTHER

(Tries to hinder the WOODCUTTER.)

Not the twins! Not the boys!

MAYA

Sunnam, my daughter. He is coming your way.
Run! Run away! Hurry!

MAYA'S face freezes with fear as she looks at the
WOODCUTTER.

MAYA screams sharply, loses consciousness, and falls.

The sounds of the wind and the window screen vibrating fade.

MAYA and the WOODCUTTER are released from the JADE
EMPEROR'S magical trance.

MAYA

(Lays still on the ground.)

People say the crime is guilty, not the man. They
say I must not hate Father, that I should forgive
him. I understand it because I know he loved me
as his daughter. But the sounds of that night—
the wind, Mother's screams—I can't stop hearing
them in my head!

MAYA closes her eyes.

Act Five

SCENE 1

The Heavenly Maiden's Home: "False Impressions"

SULHWA, the HEAVENLY MAIDEN SNOWFLOWER, is doing laundry in her courtyard with her sisters, HEAVENLY MAIDEN 1 and HEAVENLY MAIDEN 2, helping.

HEAVENLY MAIDEN 1

I'm so glad you are feeling better.

SULHWA

The medicine Maya brings from the Earth has been helpful. I feel much lighter with it.

HEAVENLY MAIDEN 1

Right. You should regain health, so Maya can heal too.

SULHWA

My Maya? She went to bed early, saying she had some body aches, but when I woke up early this morning, she was busy eating.

(*Laughs.*)

Such a hearty eater, that one.

HEAVENLY MAIDEN 2

(*Cautiously.*)

So, she's okay?

SULHWA

She seemed fine when she left this morning.

HEAVENLY MAIDEN 2

Where did she go? To testify to the Jade
Emperor again?

SULHWA

To help her brothers with archery . . .
(*Pauses.*)
Wait, what did you just say?

HEAVENLY MAIDEN 1

(*Slightly panicked.*)

Oh, nothing.

HEAVENLY MAIDEN 1 stops HEAVENLY MAIDEN 2
from speaking.

HEAVENLY MAIDEN 2

(Muttering.)

Now where did she go after making all that fuss?

HEAVENLY MAIDEN 1

(With some difficulty.)

Sulhwa, you know, I've wanted to ask you about that day . . .

SULHWA

What day? Come on, just spill it out. What are you trying to say?

HEAVENLY MAIDEN 1

I know this is years too late, but on that last day, we bathed together on Earth . . .

SULHWA pauses and puts her work down.

HEAVENLY MAIDEN 1 (CONT'D)

It was not our intention to leave you all alone in the mountain spring. We have all been feeling so badly about what happened that we could not bring it up to you to talk about it.

HEAVENLY MAIDEN 2

It was hard for us too, when you did not come back. We thought you would eventually return, perhaps just a little late, after finding your winged robe.

HEAVENLY MAIDEN 1

You know how harsh the punishment can be if we don't meet the curfew to return to the heavens.

SULHWA

Yes, I know very well. That's why I tried my best to understand you all. But why are you bringing this up now?

HEAVENLY MAIDEN 2

Because we have been called by Jade Emperor to testify about what happened that day. He summoned every *Sun-Nyeo* who was in that bath that day to your daughter's trial.

SULHWA

(Shocked.)

What?

HEAVENLY MAIDEN 2

You don't know? Maya didn't say anything?

HEAVENLY MAIDEN 1

You really had no idea what Maya has been up to?

SULHWA

No, my goodness! Please, tell me everything!

HEAVENLY MAIDEN 2

The Woodcutter and his mother were called to the trial. We heard that Maya was screaming about how both did terrible things to you and even fainted. When she revived, she told the Jade Emperor that his mandating curfew for us *Sun-Nyeos* was why her mom was left behind that day. It was his fault, too.

HEAVENLY MAIDEN 1

I mean, she's not wrong. But maybe she went a bit too far.

SULHWA

(Eyes well up with tears.)
Oh, Maya . . .

HEAVENLY MAIDEN 2

I am afraid we may get in trouble at the court for having a spirited and ungrateful niece.

HEAVENLY MAIDEN 1

Sulhwa, do you know how hard we looked for you? When we finally found you, you seemed happy living down there. We felt relieved.

SULHWA

You looked for me?

HEAVENLY MAIDEN 1

Of course! Desperately.

SULHWA

And you found me, then you left me again?

HEAVENLY MAIDEN 2

Yes, it was a lot of hard work to find you.

SULHWA

(Says with difficulty.)

If you found me, you should have at least talked to me. You should have let me know you were there and asked how I was doing.

HEAVENLY MAIDEN 1

He seemed like a nice man with kind eyes. The Woodcutter, I mean. Your baby was so cute, too. We decided it would be best not to interrupt your happy life on Earth.

SULHWA
(Shakes violently.)
I waited for you, sisters, for so long.

HEAVENLY MAIDEN 1
We thought that too at first, but you
seemed so happy.

HEAVENLY MAIDEN 2
(Speaking freely.)
Speaking of, why did you leave the Woodcutter?
I was always so curious. He is so romantic. He
loved you so much that he came all the way up
here to the heavens looking for you that time! He
braved himself for love, risking his life, getting in
that magical well bucket. I was honestly jealous
of your luck at love! I could not understand why
you'd leave such a loving husband. Why did you?
Why is Maya doing all this?

HEAVENLY MAIDEN 1
*(Tries to stop HEAVENLY MAIDEN
2's yammering.)*
Sulhwa, what did happen down there?

SULHWA

(Looks hopeless.)

Now you want to hear what happened? After all
this time? I don't want to think about that time.
Please leave. I need to lie down.

HEAVENLY MAIDEN 1 and HEAVENLY MAIDEN 2 appear
awkward, and don't know what to do.

MAYA enters holding a bow, walking lively.

MAYA

(Smiling.)

Hi Aunties, you are all here.

SULHWA

(Hides her misery.)

Good to have you back. Where are your brothers?

MAYA

They said they wanted to play a bit longer by
themselves. They are complaining that they
hate archery.

MAYA laughs.

HEAVENLY MAIDEN 2

(Sarcastically.)

You've been busy lately.

MAYA

(Observes SULHWA'S face.)

Umma, what is it? You look pale.

(Touches SULHWA'S hand.)

And your body is so cold?

SULHWA

Tell me what you've been doing lately. What's been going on?

MAYA

Umma . . .

SULHWA

Speak now!

HEAVENLY MAIDEN 1 and HEAVENLY MAIDEN 2 hurriedly exit.

SULHWA

What were you thinking? You sued who?

MAYA

(*Pauses.*)

It's all because of me.

SULHWA

What is?

MAYA

Had I not been born, you would have been able
to escape from that awful home.
(*Starts to cry.*)
Or, if I weren't a girl, Grandmother wouldn't have
been so mean to you.

SULHWA

Don't say that, Maya.

MAYA

You would have had a much better life on Earth if
it weren't for me!

SULHWA

(*Hugs MAYA.*)
No, no, it's not you. None of this is your fault.

MAYA

I saw everything, *Umma*. After giving birth to
the twins, you climbed naked onto the roof and
danced in the middle of the day.

SULHWA

What? How do you remember so long ago?

MAYA

I was so scared watching you jumping up and
down and dance, naked. Everyone was worried
that you would do it again, so nobody mentioned
it afterward. Grandmother called you a crazy bitch
and said her crazy daughter-in-law was ruining
her family.

SULHWA

Oh baby, I didn't know you saw it all and
remembered. I am so, so sorry! Back then,
I thought, maybe if I performed toward the
heavens, someone up there would see me and
come get me. I was out of my senses then, trying
to pray to the sky. I was offering a prayer to the
heavens, not craziness.

MAYA

(Starts to cry, childlike.)

I was afraid that I would lose my mind someday like you. I was scared.

SULHWA

(Holds MAYA tight, crying.)

My poor baby girl, my poor Maya. I had no idea you felt like this. I was a stupid, undeserving mother to depend on the medicine you brought.

MAYA

(Pushes SULHWA away and speaks in earnest.)

Umma, why didn't you escape sooner? Why did you do nothing all this time, all the while blaming the Jade Emperor and your sisters? When Father came to the heavens in that well bucket, looking for you, why did you let him in? Why? You kept saying you had to endure it all for your children. I had to do something! But there is nothing I can do!

MAYA cries bitterly.

SULHWA

(*Embraces MAYA without speaking for a
long time.*)
Maya, look at me and listen.

MAYA and SULHWA look into each other's eyes.

SULHWA (CONT'D)
I have never, not once, regretted having you. I was
always grateful to have you as my daughter. As a
baby, and now as a growing girl. You shared your
stories from your heart here—
(*Points to MAYA'S heart.*)
—and my own stories are here—
(*Points to her own heart.*)
Thank you for sharing from your heart. Now I
understand what needs to be done. I will finish
this trial; you need to trust me. Do you hear me?

MAYA looks at SULHWA and nods, eyes peaceful.

MAYA and SULHWA hug each other and wipe each other's tears.

Act Six

SCENE 1

The Heavenly Courtroom: Sulhwa Enters the Trial

The WOODCUTTER, GRANDMOTHER, DEER,
HEAVENLY MAIDEN 1, and HEAVENLY MAIDEN 2 all wait
for the JADE EMPEROR, talking inaudibly among themselves.

Music plays as SULHWA, wearing a beautiful winged robe,
enters, appearing determined and strong. Lights illuminate every
part of her SULHWA'S body.

ALL are speechless witnessing her entrance.

The music becomes louder, and the JADE EMPEROR enters.

ALL take their seats to resume the trial.

Act Seven

EPILOGUE

In Maya's Dream: Putting Down the Burden

The JADE EMPEROR stands centerstage.

SULHWA enters carrying a water bucket, cautious not to spill and stands close to the JADE EMPEROR.

The WOODCUTTER enters, carrying his mother on his back with difficulty, and stands on the other side of the JADE EMPEROR.

MAYA enters, struggling to drag a sack that is too large and heavy for her to manage.

MAYA cannot figure out where to stand before ultimately standing behind SULHWA.

The JADE EMPEROR stands behind the WOODCUTTER and puts his hands on GRANDMOTHER'S shoulders.

GRANDMOTHER climbs down from the WOODCUTTER's back and stands next to the WOODCUTTER.

The faces of GRANDMOTHER and WOODCUTTER relax.

The JADE EMPEROR gestures at HEAVENLY MAIDEN 1 and HEAVENLY MAIDEN 2, and they approach SULHWA, helping her put down the heavy water bucket.

SULHWA's strained body relaxes.

The JADE EMPEROR exits the scene.

MAYA inches into the space between SULHWA and the WOODCUTTER where the JADE EMPEROR formerly stood.

MAYA sits under SULHWA'S feet.

SULHWA looks at the WOODCUTTER.

The WOODCUTTER looks back at SULHWA.

SULHWA

(*Lovingly.*)
Maya, my darling daughter.

WOODCUTTER

(*Kindly.*)
My daughter Maya.

SULHWA

You finally found where you belong.

WOODCUTTER

Now let go of your burden and give it to us.

MAYA

This is too heavy. I will just keep it.

SULHWA

Umma is strong. You can give it to me.

WOODCUTTER

The burden doesn't belong to you. Give it to me;
your father is strong, too.

SULHWA

We will take your burden now.

WOODCUTTER

We will take care of this now.

MAYA

Then what will I carry? I am afraid I will disappear
if this burden disappears.

SULHWA

Maya, you've been carrying the burden, but you are not the burden.

WOODCUTTER

Drop the burden and take our love and resilience with you instead. Now you can go live your own life.

SULHWA

(Gesturing offstage.)
Now you can be free and go live.

MAYA

(Hesitating.)
Can I really do that?

JADE EMPEROR

(Approaches MAYA affectionately.)
Maya, what do you wish to do with that burden?

MAYA

There is a lot packed in here. I want to unpack them one by one and throw them away.

JADE EMPEROR

Oh, that sounds good. Go ahead.

MAYA unties the knot of the heavy sack.

Inside the sack are many bundles of clothes in different colors. MAYA opens the bundles one by one and throws them away, her hands working faster.

There is a sound of wind.

The colorful clothes opened and started to rise and dance around MAYA in the wind.

MAYA stands and starts dancing around with the fabrics like a playful, innocent child.

SULHWA
There, go live your life, dancing, just like that.

WOODCUTTER
Remember, we are here to support you, always.

GRANDMOTHER
Don't look back, my dear. Just keep going.

JADE EMPEROR
Maya, keep moving forward.

Happy music plays as MAYA keeps dancing joyfully.

END.

Playwright's Note: What do you imagine Sulhwa, the Heavenly Maiden, did at the trial in the heavenly court? How will Maya's life be different now with a mother who has taken her power back? Perhaps you can write that story yourselves—I would love to hear all the stories from you, respected readers. I hope each of your stories of hope can reach the world like raindrops, like snowflakes, and I happily leave this playwright's pen with you.

About Youngmi Baek-Youn

Youngmi Baek-Youn, once dreamed of being an actor as a child, now lives her life as a play-writing therapist. She runs a private practice and workshops as the CEO of Center for Women's Growth and Healing, dedicated to assisting those suffering from trauma through their healing journey. Since debuting as a play-wright with "Let's Get a Job," a play supporting the labor rights of teens, she has continued to write numerous plays for participants of her educational drama and drama therapy workshops. She has also translated several books such as Internal Family Systems Guide to Recovery from Eating Disorders, The Shadow King, *and* Motherpeace — A Way to the Goddess through Myth, Art, and Tarot.

the Story of the Feminist who Rewrote the Story

The Hidden Story Behind the Heavenly Maiden and Woodcutter Folktale

The main character is Maya

Three children are in this story of the Heavenly Maiden and the Woodcutter. The eldest of the three, Maya, is the protagonist in this rewrite. Maya is a character that represents countless women I have met in therapeutic settings and reflects my own life. I wrote this in a play format, as an open-ended courtroom trial. This way, you, the reader, may participate in the writing of the ending and act as one of the jurors. I ask you to consider a few things for your fair participation and judgment.

Justice — Different Perspectives

First, I ask everyone to be just in their decisions. In the past 15 years, I have met varying populations, from teenagers to those in their 60s, and have led them on adult educational therapy and feminist psychodrama, during which we restructured this folktale from the Heavenly Maiden's perspective. Some participants have been victims of rape and domestic violence, and some were educators who work to prevent gender-based crimes. In almost all of these sessions, at least one or two people have said something like this:

"The Heavenly Maiden is a selfish and cold-hearted woman who broke the Woodcutter's heart and left without looking back. I feel bad for the Woodcutter, not to mention the children

who got separated from their father. She didn't even consider what was best for the kids—she destroyed her family.

"There must be a reason why she was left behind and did not get help from other Heavenly Maidens when she lost her winged robe. She was either an antisocial loner or an arrogant snob who got what she deserved."

We need to rethink how we define justice. Let's imagine there are two different images that both represent "justice."

In one image, on the top, a stone chair is in the middle between two pillars. An authority figure is sitting on the chair, wearing a golden crown and a colorful robe decorated with jewels. The authority figure holds a sword in one hand and a balance scale in the other. The person in the image seems calm, logical, and unaffected by deep human emotions.

Now, let's turn to the image on the bottom. There are three goddesses surrounding a large tree. All the goddesses communicate with all living beings. The goddess in the center has her hand on the root of the tree, and the other hand is holding a crystal near her chest, which seems to be connected to the core of Earth energy. She connects to the Earth's core energy by sitting on Earth with one hand on the tree's root and the other on a crystal at her heart. The goddess on the right is giving water to the tree while feeling the breadth of the tree with the other hand. She provides water to the tree and feels the breath of the tree, listening and responding to every living being. The third goddess on the left is reaching out her hand to a deer as if to ask what the animal needs. The deer responds on behalf of all animals, including humans.

Did that description paint the pictures well in your mind's eye? In your opinion, which card looks more just?

The image on the top is the traditional Rider Waite tarot card for justice, and the image on the bottom is the justice card from the feminist tarot deck called Motherpeace. Which of the two cards conveys the message, "Justice is not served until all beings, including myself, are happy, healthy, and peaceful"? The correct answer is the Motherpeace tarot card.

Among people who fight for justice, of right vs. wrong, many tend to see things in a simple black-or-white mindset and have difficulty interpreting a situation from multiple perspectives. From the patriarchal perspective that has permeated into our inner narratives and outer world, the story of the Heavenly Maiden and the Woodcutter is a sad romantic story of a man in love. Very few perceived this story as a psychological thriller about a man's obsession to possess and control a woman he loved.

Some people were uncomfortable even employing the Heavenly Maiden's point of view in the story. Perhaps they were afraid they would find something they would rather not see. For these folklores to survive through the generations of a patriarchal society full of gender-based crimes, only small hints of the woman's point of view would need to remain in the story. Perhaps they were hoping someday their descendants would uncover their unspoken, hidden side of the story.

If we were to approach the situation from multiple perspectives, it is not difficult to understand why the Heavenly Maiden had to return to the heavens with her young children. Only when we can see all the things—personal, political, conscious, subconscious, spoken words, and bodily communications—we are able to see all the beings as they are. That is if you become curious about the internal reality aside from the external, visible one.

Acknowledging the pain through deep empathy

Secondly, I ask that you open your heart to those who stand trial, shaking with trauma and pain, asking to be heard. Society and culture affect an individual; in turn, the individual influences and shapes society and culture. Since everything is connected in this manner, each individual reflects the society and the culture. Therefore, when someone opens up about their pain, we can share their experience and support their healing. In my adult gender study programs, we process this with a discussion. The discussion topic is this:

"Who is responsible for the Heavenly Maiden's tragic life in which she was forced to live according to someone else's agenda and wishes, isolated from all she was familiar with? Let's apply the legal standards of modern times to discuss."

When the discussion started, there was inevitably a point of view that said, "Why do we always make a woman victim when the real world is full of women's oppression already?" This usually leads to the group rewriting the story as the Heavenly Maiden becomes a superhero. With this game-changing suggestion, we created exciting scenarios where the Heavenly Maiden could protect herself with her superhuman strength and her martial art skills and where the other Heavenly Maidens show their love for their sisters with

their heroic powers. It felt vindicating! Yet while the other participants were focused on feeling good about solving this problem,
the participant playing the role of the Heavenly Maiden expressed
feeling isolated and lonely. Everyone was so interested in solving
the problem that they failed to acknowledge or empathize with the
trauma or pain the Heavenly Maiden had experienced.

In the rewrite of the story, Sulhwa, the Heavenly Maiden, and
her daughter Maya perhaps stood trial because they wanted their
pain acknowledged. I hope that you realize that serving true justice
is not only determining right and wrong but also opening your
heart to listen and empathize with the pains of the vulnerable.

Generational Trauma and Mother Wound

Third, it is essential to understand the intergenerational trauma
passed down from generation to generation. What environment
could the three children be born and raised in? How would they
have thought and felt about two different worlds, Heaven and
Earth? Perhaps they felt conflicted between the two cultures, or
one took precedence over the other. A similar process could occur
internally in the children's minds, making it difficult for them to
feel whole. If we look into how an individual interacts with the
previous generation or the next generation within the familial community, we can find the source of one's trauma or pain. I hope you
consider this fact as you look into the dynamics of Maya's family.

To survive, children tend to look to the primary caregiver and
absorb their emotions like a sponge. They feel the caregiver's body
temperature, changes in facial expression, breath, and heartbeat
and respond in the best way they can. At one point, we were one

united body within our mothers' bodies. Not just during that time, but after leaving the mother's body and passing through infancy, and as we pass through stages of development, we share many emotions without clearly knowing where the mothers' feelings end and where ours begin.

When children are entirely dependent on the caregiver, the caregiver's unhappiness is a definite threat to the children. Particularly when the caregiver is isolated and experiences loneliness and a sense of deficit, her attachment to her child increases exponentially. Children take in this situation promptly and try very hard to make her sad feelings disappear. They may feel helpless at being unable to do so, and they may develop a desire to grow up fast to help their caregiver. At the very least, they try to smile so the caregiver can, too.

When children grow, they become experts at making their caregivers happy. They help around the house, look after their younger siblings, perform well in school, and act satisfied while hiding their sad feelings. Every time they do, they receive praise and reinforcement, which encourages children to try even harder to become someone their caregivers can be proud of. Before long, they will realize how they have grown to guard their caregivers' emotions without thinking. This is the communal dependency that is created by intergenerational trauma.

In psychotherapy, those surrounding themselves with people who need them are known as codependent individuals. I would like to help the readers' understanding of codependency at this time.

In this story, Maya also becomes her mother's protector and fights the injustices in the world. She feels anger against her father and his family for making her mother depressed and cry. She feels full of rage and is motivated to seek justice. This makes her view all the powers in the world as unjust because she has never experienced just authority.

Many daughters in this world, just like Maya, fight to right the wrong in their mother's past instead of trying to live their own lives and move forward. Gradually, daughters feel overburdened. They feel sad for the mothers who they need to protect, and at the same time, they blame their mothers for leaving such pain to carry. They feel frustrated and unhappy with reality, but by this time, they are stuck and unable to escape. They are frightened that the minute they stop doing what they have been doing, their lives will crumble and fall.

This sense of being afraid stems from a young inner voice inside one's consciousness. One recent client mentioned that because she was so worried about her father being violent with her mother, she used all her accumulated sick leave to follow them on a trip overseas. Codependency is activated to overcome the mental burden and anxiety.

However, there are various voices within our internal minds. One of them keeps talking—the voice of an ego that wants to be psychologically independent! As this ego gets activated during puberty, it starts to feel something is wrong. In the internal mind of the daughters, all different voices fight with one another. Sometimes they find a way to compromise—like living for someone other than their mothers. This could be their friends, romantic partners, spouse, or spiritual leaders. However, just because the recipient has changed doesn't mean that the way of their living has changed. The daughter's role in the relationship remains. They still expect reinforcement and acknowledgment.

As I have done this work for many years, I have frequently heard from many clients who say, "I am afraid I would disappear if I stop playing this role." However, we all have our roles and responsibilities in this intergenerational pain. The parents' share of duties should be their own responsibility, not the children's.

The problem is that neither the parent nor the child knows where their responsibility starts and ends. The vicious cycle continues. To end this vicious cycle, I utilize "family building" exercises as one of the psychotherapy models. This story also reflects the principle of family building exercise.

Sulhwa, Maya's mother, walks into the trial, determined to end the pain shared with her daughter. I have seen such faces during the past 20 years as I worked with survivors of domestic violence. Even though they had no choice but to succumb to violence, these women realize that they are strong survivors rather than victims, and to ensure that their pain and trauma are not passed down to their children, these heroines are determined to be strong and independent. Through therapy, I have seen countless *Sun-Nyeos* who shed their pain and put on their winged robe to fly. There was hope. These *Sun-Nyeos* made sure their babies knew of their mother's love and strength so that their children wouldn't have to have sleepless nights worrying about them. These winged robes represented the ability to endure a long, difficult divorce trial, overcome the fear of knives caused by their husband's threats, become financially independent, or learn professional skills. One became an owner of a restaurant, and another became a therapist for the survivors of domestic violence.

Wounded Warriors like Maya

Lastly, we need to look into caring for Maya's inner world, similar to the inner world of other warriors fighting against patriarchy and injustice. Some feminists have attempted mirroring techniques to demonstrate the brutality of patriarchal thought and behaviors. They found the method exhilarating and hoped it would raise awareness of societal problems.

Because the original scenarios were brutal, those who mirrored them were also violent. Unfortunately, the public criticized these mirroring warriors instead of the actual perpetrators. People criticized, "How can women be that violent? They are worse than men. They are promoting misogyny, not eradicating it."

As a feminist and a psychotherapist, my primary concern was these mirror-warriors' well-being. They seemed like warriors fighting at the forefront with nothing but a mirror to protect them. They were intelligent, resilient, and brilliant. But the warriors had to be always on high alert for the original perpetrators and often had to ignore the cyberbullying or icy criticism from the public. On this battlefield, there is no room for depression, anxiety, or helplessness. The warriors cannot afford to show their vulnerability. They cannot be hurt by negative comments on the internet. The only acceptable emotion for these warriors was anger. As this continued, the warriors' hearts also grew cold. On the other side of the mirror, their souls were bleeding.

Maya's inner world was just like this. There was always so much chaos and conflict in her inner world. All her segmented egos were in conflict with one another and unable to unite harmoniously. Some of these egos are oblivious to their roles, purposes, or presence. Maya was always angry, but a sense of helplessness was underneath that anger. Maya experiences dual, opposing emotions in almost everything she encounters, e.g., hating the person who hurt her while wishing to understand and forgive them. Wanting to place blame on someone vs. blaming herself for everything. Being motivated to do everything perfectly vs. not wanting to do anything. Wanting to caretake someone vs. feeling burdened by it. Maya also deeply resents the male gender while feeling disappointed for being born a female gender.

The inner pairs that are at odds with one another ignore and blame the other. These polarized conflicts can be experienced by many people. The appropriate amount of polarization brings balance and peace. Still, when polarization is too extreme, the quality of life suffers and affects all aspects of work and personal life.

Maya has a secret that no one else knows. One is her bulimia, and another is her deep sense of shame because of it. The "Inner Antagonist," which is independent and driven, leads Maya to rebel against society's injustice, but the "Inner Patriarch" that resides deep within her psyche blames Maya for her dangerous behaviors that disrupt the community.

This intense internal conflict creates pain, enabling another ego that tries to numb this pain. This ego forces her attention to the external world so that she can locate comfort. To Maya, this was food. From a very young age, she felt empty as she was mothering her own mother as a child, never fully embodying herself.

Maya is unable to distinguish the emotional and physical hunger. As long as Maya only focuses on her eating behavior and weight, all her attempts to escape the eating disorder will fail miserably. Unless the primary source of her pain is resolved, the internal war and the bulimic behavior will continue to return.

Above all, Maya must be understanding and compassionate with all her egos. It is time that she should pay attention to their intentions, fears, and desires. While she has lived an admirable life fighting for the weak and vulnerable, she must also realize that she is included in the group she needs to care for.

Dear readers, please remember what Maya needs to learn to heal and grow. Now, shall we start rewriting this story together? I hope you come up with a story that is just and wise. Let's begin with:

"Not too long ago, a Heavenly Maiden and a Woodcutter had a daughter."

We dedicate this play to the survivors of domestic violence and their children.

Divided Women in the Dangun Myth: Bear Woman & Tiger Woman

This appendix is edited from the paper published in 1991 by Sookyeol Ryu, "Divided Women in the Korean Origin Myth."

In her monumental book *The Second Sex,* Simone de Beauvoir wrote, "One is not born but rather becomes a woman." Women have long been treated inferior to men in almost all societies worldwide. Korean society is not an exception. Since I started exploring women with a feminist approach, I have been curious about how the women of Korea became "Korean women," asking questions like:

- Who are "Korean women"?[18]
- How did they come to such an identity?
- Who am I?
- Who are my sisters?
- Where did we start?

---

18)   A stereotype of Korean women as defined as the norm or just by the traditional Korean society.

My studies into the history of Korea's women led me to Ung-Nyeo, the Bear Woman, the figure cited as the very first Korean woman.

In my long quest to understand how Korean society creates the archetype of the Korean woman, I realized I must go back to the beginning, all the way to the creation myth of ancient Korea. There, I could identify the very first Korean woman: Ung-Nyeo, the Bear Woman from the Dangun Myth.

The following is the myth from *Samguk Yusa:*

Here is what we know from ancient history.

A long time ago, Hwan-In knew that his *suhja*[19] son Hwan-Ung was interested in the human world under the sky. He looked down around Mt. Taebaeksan and saw an appropriate place to build a kingdom from which he could reign. So he sent Hwan-Ung down with three Chunbu-in.

Hwan-Ung descended to Taebaeksan with a group of three thousand people and established his city. This is the divine king Hwan-Ung. He ruled all matters of wind, rain, and clouds while managing and teaching 360 tasks of the human world. These included matters of farming, birth, illness and healing, laws and penalties, and good and evil.

Around this time, a bear and a tiger lived together in a cave and asked Hwan-Ung to help them become human. He gave them each a bundle of sacred mugwort and 20 pieces of sacred garlic, saying, "If you eat only this for 100 days without seeing sunlight,

---

19)   An illegitimate son, a son of a concubine or son who is not a direct heir.

you will receive a human body." The bear and tiger received them. The bear transformed into a woman 21 days later, but the tiger did not follow the sacred rule and did not receive a human body.

Ung-Nyeo did not have anyone to marry, so she prayed to become pregnant at Shindansoo, the sacred altar tree. Hwan-Ung temporarily took on a human form to marry Ung-Nyeo, and together they had a son. He was named Dangun Wang-gum.

Ung-Nyeo in the myth appears in *Samguk Yusa*, one of Korea's two oldest historical books. It was written by a monk named Il Yeon in the Goryeo period, around 1270 CE, when Buddhism was most prevalent. The book includes segments of stories from various sources that no longer exist today and details Korea's indigenous beliefs and folk traditions. Therefore, in a way, the real value of *Samguk Yusa* is not a historical one but rather a mythical one.

The historian Shin Chae-ho who published the *Ancient History of Joseon* in 1948, criticized the heavy influence of ancient Chinese ideology and Confucianism in the ways Korean myths were written. It is interesting to see what Shin Chae-ho pointed out about gender inequality in Korea's ancient myths. He wrote:

It is very well known that women were respected equally in the early years of the Three Kingdoms era. However, in these myths, the men are depicted as divine, whereas the women are portrayed as animals. Because of such degradation of women, Samguk Yusa seems like a byproduct of Buddhist embellishment rather than the original form of the myth.

In the book *A Bibliographical Introduction to Samguk Yusa*, written by Choi Nam-sun in 1927, *Samguk Yusa* is recognized as one of the best resources for retrieving Korea's past. The way Choi Nam-sun approached history is quite intriguing. It is known that he has said these words to his followers in the 1930s:

History cannot, and should not be, regarded as a science without heart because it is learning for the sake of the people. Historical studies should have purpose and emotion behind them.

Moreover, by relating the myth to Korean Shamanism, Choi made a decisive contribution to the understanding of the myth. After linking the story to the shaman-ruling society of ancient Korea, for instance, he concluded that Dangun, the founder of Korean civilization, was actually the shaman-ruler. This interpretation has since been accepted by most scholars of later generations and has served as the baseline for the analysis of the myth.

The Ambivalent God, Hwan-Ung

Up to this point, the existing studies on the Dangun Myth were focused on the main male protagonists. Considering the patriarchal background of Korean society, this is not all that surprising. In this myth, there are three male protagonists present: Hwan-In (the highest God in the high sky), Hwan-Ung (Hwan-In's son that descends to the Earth), and Dangun (Hwan-Ung's son that becomes the founding father for the Koreans). Because this myth explains how the country was built, it is considered the founding myth of Korea.

In his published research on the Dangun Myth, Choi Nam-sun interprets the myth based on linguistic analysis and folklore stories. He highlighted the concept of *"tangeuri"* in Mongolian folklore. Choi also stated that the key to understanding the Dangun Myth is in his name, "Dangun." He believed that the name derived from the ancient Korean words *taegari* (태가리)" or *"tagal* (태갈)," which sound similar to the Mongolian word *"tangeuri."* In Altaic languages, including the Korean language, *tangeuri* or *tongol* in Mongolian means "the sky" or "shaman."

Moreover, words such as *Dangol* (당골) or *Dangoleh* (당골래) continued to refer to a shaman in various areas of modern Korea, at least until the 1900s. In modern Korean, *daegari* (대가리) means "the head." Choi was certain that *Dangun* was the name of the ancient Korean Shaman ruler and argued that the Dangun Myth was a byproduct of an ancient Korean society with Shamanism at its core.

In the myth, Hwan-In is the highest God of the sky and the grandfather of Dangun. *Hwan* refers to the light or the brightness, and *In* refers to the beginning or the origin. Thus, the name signals that everything originates from him: he is the Source, the Divine. His son, Hwan-Ung, shares the divine name of "Hwan" with his father, but his name is "Ung," which refers simply to *male.* Therefore, we know that the first God to descend from the sky to Earth was male.

In the original myth, the term used to describe Hwan-Ung was *suhja* (서자), which meant *illegitimate son of an unmarried woman* or *son of a concubine*—in other words, a male who cannot be a direct heir. Disturbed by this, many Korean scholars participated in discussions around the issue. Most scholars in this debate concluded that *suhja* must not mean *an illegitimate son* but *one who was not the eldest son*. They argued that earthly relationships cannot be directly applied to the gods in the heavens. What the Korean scholars accomplished via this debate was to reinstate Hwan-Ung's status as the legitimate son of a first wife rather than the son of a concubine.

The privileges that the eldest son enjoys come from a long tradition of the Joseon Dynasty and are still prevalent in contemporary Korean society. The first son receives the biggest inheritance and carries on the family lineage. The traditional *Hoju* system remained in effect until 2004, giving special status and power to only the eldest son as the head of the family line. A son's status was determined based on the order in which he was born and by which mother he was born from. How the first wife and the concubines were distinguished affected the sons' lives in several ways. During the Joseon era, the sons and the descendants of the concubines were prohibited from taking government exams, therefore blocking them from the place of political fame and power.

I believe the whole debate about Hwan-Ung's being the legitimate or illegitimate son is pointless. In my view, the fact that Hwan-Ung came down to Earth to rule clarifies the hierarchy between the heavens and earth. Hwan-Ung's position is clearly below Hwan-In, the highest God of the sky, and above the animals, such as bears and tigers, who wanted to be humans. His descent to the Earth needs justification, so regardless of whether he was an illegitimate son, it was imperative that Hwan-Ung have an inferior status to the sons that remained in the sky.

However, he is still pictured as the divine presence that governs all aspects of human life and is differentiated from other humans. He can control the wind, the rain, and the snow, all of which are essential elements in agriculture. To Koreans, the wind and the water were the most important natural elements. Korean people developed a unique philosophy of feng shui. Combined with ancestor worship, feng shui was comparable to religion during the Goryeo era, and even to this day, this belief persists strongly among Korean people.

The Dangun Myth does not talk about the hunter-gatherers, the primitive way of survival for the human species; it only talks about farming. Therefore, we can assume that when the Dangun Myth was formed, the ancient society was based on agriculture and that it already contained the fundamental belief systems handed down to future generations.

The text does not define the three amulets that Hwan-Ung received before he descended from the sky. Some scholars hypothesized that these would be shamanic instruments like the ceremonial sword, the sacred mirror, and the shamanic rattle. Others argued that the third amulet was probably a crown or a drum rather than a rattle. The five main aspects of Hwan-Ung's rule included farming, birth, illness and healing, laws and penalties, and good and evil. However, the text also says that Hwan-Ung oversaw 360 elements that affected human life in addition to these five. As 360 is the number of days in the lunar calendar year, this most likely means that Hwan-Ung oversaw everything that happened in human life every day to make human life better.

The structure of the Dangun Myth includes three generations

of divine males: Hwan-In (the God of the sky), Hwan-Ung (the God of the Earth), and Dangun (the human). Kim Mu-jo, another historian in modern times, argued that while these three men may have different names, they are all one and the same, thereby completing the holy trinity. Kim Mu-jo also discussed the Korean people's beliefs in Samshin, the Goddess of fertility in indigenous Korean culture and folklore, and connected this deity to the three divine men listed above.

According to the Korean-English dictionary currently used in modern Korean society, Samshin has two meanings: one refers to the three gods from the myth that founded Korea, and the other refers to the goddess Samshin who governs fertility, pregnancy, and childbirth. Koreans usually refer to the latter as the Grandmother Samshin. However, Kim Mu-jo argues that Samshin is the creatrix god of all humanity because it is the identity of the three gods where everything began.

In Korea, the goddess that governs pregnancy and childbirth is viewed as being female, as the name Grandmother Samshin demonstrates. If we were to accept that the three gods (Hwan-In, Hwan-Ung, and Dangun) are the gods of pregnancy and birth, then this presents a fundamental problem with the feminine trait of Samshin. To solve this problem, Kim Mu-jo focuses on the fact that in the myth, Dangun, the son of Ung-Nyeo, became a mountain god after he died. According to the myth, Dangun ruled for 1,908 years and then headed to the mountains to become a mountain god.

The most prevalent image of a mountain god (Sanshin) in Korean folklore is an old man with a long, white beard. However, according to historians, this patriarchal appearance of the mountain god was created only after the influx of Chinese Confucian philosophy. In historical artifacts, it is known that many mountains had female names, such as those of *Mt. Daemo* (Great Mother), *Mt. Moak* (Mother's Hill), *Mt. Sun-Nyeo* (Heavenly Maiden), *Mt. Jamo* (Kind Mother), *Mt. Mohu* (Generous Mother), and *Mt. Moho* (Mother's Protection). Also, in Korean Shamanism, the indigenous religion of Korea, the mountain gods were originally female. Therefore, Kim Mu-jo is saying that after Dangun died, he became a mountain god: a female goddess of fertility. He argues the three gods: Hwan-In, Hwan-Ung, and Dangun, equate to the Samshin goddess.

I find Kim Mu-jo's studies connecting the Dangun Myth with that of the fertility goddess Samshin very insightful. That said, I find it problematic that he unconditionally equated the three male gods to the female fertility goddess without much explanation. Gerda Lerner, the feminist historian, attributes such phenomena of transferring the female goddess to a male god to the development of plow agriculture:

Agriculture, coinciding with increasing militarism, brought major changes in kinship and in gender relations, so did the development of strong kingships and archaic states bring changes in religious beliefs and symbols. The observable pattern is: first, the demotion of the Mother-Goddess figure and the ascendance and later dominance of her male consort/son; then his merging with a storm-god into a male Creator-God, who heads the pantheon of gods and goddesses. Wherever such changes occur, the power of creation of fertility is transferred from the Goddess to the God.

As I studied the Dangun Myth and wrote this thesis, I could not help but think about how this myth may be connected to the worshipping of the Korean fertility goddess. As Gerda Lerner presumed, the patriarchal transformation of the female goddess into the male god may have taken place in the case of the Ung-Nyeo Myth, and the written form of the myth represents the patriarchal domination in Korea. However, considering that the text is the oldest written record of the myth, after several invasions by countries like China and Japan destroyed much of Korea's cultural assets, it is impossible to imagine the original form of the myth.

In various types of Shamanism, it is believed the universe consists of Heaven, Earth, and the Underworld, connected by a central axis. This axis is the gate or portal by which the gods descend to the Earth. The underlying idea is the belief in the possibility of direct communication with Heaven. The most widespread mythical images of the "Center of the World" are those of the cosmic mountain and the world tree.

In the case of Korean Shamanism, this center of the world could be the "sacred altar tree" on top of Mt. Taebaeksan, where Hwan-Ung descended. Under this tree, the bear and the tiger prayed to become humans and the place where Ung-Nyeo prayed for a child. *Shindansoo*, the sacred altar tree that connects the three worlds of Heaven, Earth, and the Underworld, was also called *Shinshi*, the Divine City. The union of the celestial God and the earthly animal creates the first human, in the sense that the birth was of man and woman's union. Dangun, who inherited divinity from the father, and earthliness from the mother, symbolizes sovereign humankind. However, this incarnate Dangun, also symbolizes the gender hierarchy: he must stand on his mother, the dark Earth, and prop up his father, the bright Heaven.

The Transformation of the Bear into a Woman

The story of Ung-Nyeo is known as the "Dangun Myth," after her son and the founder of the Korean people. However, I believe this myth should really be titled: *the Ung-Nyeo Myth*. This is because I believe Ung-Nyeo is the main protagonist of this story, not her son. All the main progressions of the story come from Ung-Nyeo. I believe that the story's main theme is how a bear turns into a woman. Therefore, I will focus on the second part of the myth, where the transformation from animal to human occurs.

A woman's body is an interesting place that holds the secrets of primitive humans and asks questions that cannot be easily answered. Where does life come from? As the main vessel of a new life through pregnancy and childbirth, women's bodies pose a problem for men in control. That's why the origin stories of humanity often begin from a male-centered point of view, with both the man and the woman in adulthood and capable of procreating. The Korean version of the Dangun Myth is similar in distorting and negating women's power of human creation.

Let's investigate all the elements a bear needs to become human. Hwan-Ung instructed the tiger and the bear to eat only sacred mugwort and 20 garlic bulbs. To Koreans, the mugwort plant and garlic are an important part of a diet and are also considered medicine. The mugwort plant is a common herbal medicine for healing irregular periods or other menstrual ailments. It is also believed to have the power to cleanse evil spirits and energies. On the Dano holiday (May 5th of the Lunar Year), Koreans used to hang mugwort on the front door to protect against evil entering their homes.

On the other hand, garlic is known to amplify sexual stamina and therefore was prohibited among Buddhist monks who had to dedicate themselves to spiritual training suppressing physical desires. Then what could be the reason behind instructing the animals to use medicinal herbs that aid reproductive health and sex?

I believe that these ingredients were presented so that the bear and the tiger could become sexual beings. Thanks to the "sacred" medicinal plants, the bear and the tiger could transform into humans with reproductive abilities. The medicinal herbs that the bear and the tiger ate play a role in including sexual characteristics into their existence. This method, presented by Hwan-Ung, is critical in understanding the story.

Kim Yul-Gyu, another Korean mythologist, finds a reflection of the female initiation rite in the process of the bear's transformation. The essential aim of these rites is to dramatize the biological life cycle by indicating the death of childhood and the rebirth into adulthood. Mircea Eliade explained:

> *From the archaic stages of culture, the initiation of adolescents includes a series of rites whose symbolism is crystal clear: through them, the novice is first transformed into an embryo and then is reborn. Initiation is equivalent to a second birth. It is through the agency of initiation that the adolescent becomes both socially responsible and a culturally awakened being. The return to the womb is signified either by the neophyte's*

seclusion in a hut, or by a monster, or by his entering a sacred spot identified with the uterus of Mother Earth.

However, critical differences exist in the puberty rites of boys and girls. While the male rites emphasize the identity of the male with the community, the female rites focus on her subjection to sexual and biological roles. Psychologist Joseph Henderson provides an insightful explanation of the female rites of passage:

The theme of submission as an essential attitude toward promotion of the successful initiation rite can be clearly seen in the case of girls or women. Their rite of passage initially emphasizes their essential passivity, and this is reinforced by the physiological limitation on their autonomy imposed by the menstrual cycle. It has been suggested that the menstrual cycle may actually be the major part of initiation from a woman's point of view, since it has the power to awaken the deepest sense of obedience to life's creative power over her. Thus, she willingly gives herself to her womanly function, much as a man gives himself to his assigned role in the community life of his group.

There is a clear parallel between the female initiation rite and the rite of the bear and the tiger to become human. However, specific symbolisms must be understood and explained through a Korean cultural lens.

The period of seclusion Hwan-Ung initially instructed the bear and the tiger to undergo was one hundred days. Yet the bear acquired a body of a woman after only 21 days. What do these numbers signify? Because the myth's text does not explain this discordance, we can only make assumptions based on traces of various rites.

In Korea, 100 days and 21 days are both important symbols related to childbirth. Practicing 100 days of prayer to conceive a son is still a widely practiced tradition among modern Korean women. Various folklore records how women wanting to bear a son complete 100 days of prayers in the mountains, in the temples, under the trees, or in front of the big rocks.

When the baby is born, *Sam Chil Il* (*Three Times Seven Days*, thus 21 days) is the first celebration of the child's birth. Before 21 days, the baby is not technically regarded as born into this world. When the marked straw rope is hung over the front door, this means that the goddess of childbirth, the Grandmother Samshin is about to come and that no one else is allowed entry. On the 21st day, the marked rope is removed, and visitors are allowed for the first time. Therefore, at 21 days, it would be the time to announce a baby's arrival.

The amount that the bear and the tiger had to eat—one bunch of mugwort plant and 20 bulbs of garlic—comes out to be 21. Moreover, the 100-day celebration on the 100th day after birth is also one of the biggest rites of passage for a newborn, followed by the first birthday. Since both 100 days and 21 days are linked to the birth rituals of Korea, it could be said that the bear's ordeal is related to the woman's reproductive function.

If so, why did the bear become a woman after just 21 days, not after the original 100 days? If we apply a biological explanation, one may argue that even if a woman was instructed to pray for 100 days to conceive a son, she never knows when the actual conception will occur. And if she succeeds in getting pregnant, she never knows the gender. Conception and gender determination of a child were completely out of Ung-Nyeo's control in the myth.

This apparent discordance—that Hwan-Ung could instruct 100 days of prayer but does not know when those prayers will bear fruit—seems to be an intended discordance between 100 and 21. Why 21 days? Again, biologically, 21 days is when a woman could detect her pregnancy after ovulation within one month of her menstrual cycle. In this regard, the discordance of the days is a scientifically calculated one.

On the other hand, the text did not clarify whether the bear and the tiger wished to be a woman or a man. Here, another discordance arises, creating a gap in the sense that they desired to become just human, not women. According to the feminist scholar Mieke Bal, the "gap" is the spot in a text where the information is insufficient and creates a question for the readers.

As the text of the myth goes, the bear wasn't specifically interested in becoming a woman. Then why did it? This asks: *who wanted the bear to become a woman?* A possible answer is the narrator. *Who is the narrator?* The narrator of the myth is the collective mind of ancient Koreans. Let's explore whether this collective mind is female or male.

The myth says that Ung-Nyeo could not find anyone to marry after becoming human, so she prayed under the sacred altar tree to become pregnant. The first thing the bear had to do after her transformation was to find a man to marry. Here, it is still unclear whether the narrator or Ung-Nyeo wanted her to marry and have a child. According to the myth, after listening to her prayers, Hwan-Ung temporarily took a human form and married Ung-Nyeo, after which she became pregnant and gave birth to a son. Now we know that it is Hwan-Ung who gets the final product of this transformational ritual.

However, even Hwan-Ung, a god who descended from the sky, had to transform himself into a human form in order to marry. But because he was the god who "regulates all metamorphosis," he didn't have to go through the ordeal of seclusion in the dark to transform. The whole series of transformations—the prayers of the bear and the tiger, Hwan-Ung's instructions to take sacred medicinal herbs, and the seclusion in the cave without seeing the sun—are meant for a final transformation, which is Hwan-Ung's transformation into a human male. Therefore, the narrator of this text is almost equal to the story's male protagonist, Hwan-Ung. In this context, the ancient mind of the Korean people that narrated and wrote this myth is a male mind.

If we consider the fact that in real life, it is impossible for animals to turn into humans, then we can know that in ancient Korea, while there weren't any bears that turned into humans, there were actual flesh and blood women. We can assume that the bear's seclusion did not occur, either. What had instead taken place could be a marriage rite that had to be performed in a cave, in darkness.

Hwan-Ung, the god from the sky, instructed the bear to pray for 100 days to become a woman who would conceive a son. Therefore, it can be said that the hidden meaning of the 100 days of seclusion is not that a bear becomes a human but that a woman conceives a son. In other words, the ancient Korean consciousness may have utilized a bear to introduce female reproduction. In this sense, if we apply Jacques Derrida's concept of "overrun" here, the entire process of transformation is reversed. It is not that a bear became a woman, but that a woman became a bear.

Right after the marriage, the story says, "She became pregnant and bore a son." Why not a baby girl, a daughter? Why does the child have to be a boy? The reason for the boy's preference is apparent: she must have a son because he must perpetuate the family line. Thus, we can presume that a patriarchal order had already been established in old Korean society when this myth was shaped.

Female maturation was represented by an animal (the bear) changing into a human female (Ung-Nyeo), reflecting the hope that women can be safely incorporated into society to reproduce. The bear's transformation into a woman implies two rebirths: the first is that the animal becomes a human, and the second is the latter's transformation into female maturity to reproduce. The god Hwan-Ung, the story's male protagonist, directs and makes this multi-layered rebirth of the bear happen.

The Failed Tiger: The Other Woman

At first, two animals shared the same state of being animals, wanting to become human. Why is one a bear and the other a tiger? Only one of the two, the bear, succeeded in becoming a human, while the other, the tiger, failed. Why were they not of the same species—two bears or two tigers? The beliefs of Siberian and North Asiatic bear totem culture may have influenced the Korean story. The tiger is one of the most worshipped animals for Koreans, often referred to in folklore. (E.g. the 1988 Korean Seoul Olympics mascot was a tiger named Hodori.) Even in the ancient stories in *Samguk Yusa*, the tiger appears 26 times. Thus, it could be said that the tiger is a more familiar animal than the bear to ancient Koreans. Then why is the tiger, not the bear, the one to fail?

In mountainous countries, the country's collective consciousness was reflected in mountain worship. In the case of Korea, a country over 70% mountainous, the tiger, the most powerful predator in these mountains, came to be referred to as "the king of the mountains" and was also worshipped as the guardian protector spirit of the nation and ancestors. This mountain worship culture led to tiger worship culture. The symbolism of the tiger's power and bravery came to represent a core philosophy of the Korean people. As Choi Nam-sun once said, "[the] Joseon Dynasty could have been called the Tiger Dynasty considering their special bond."

In Korean folklore, the tiger usually appears as a manifestation of Sanshin, the mountain god. Tiger was the only symbol of Sanshin until the mid-Joseon era when people started painting a grandfather with white hair and a beard as Sanshin—posing an issue regarding the tiger's gender. Is the tiger male or female? Kim Mu-jo, who had researched the symbolism of the tiger as Sanshin in Korean folklore, concluded these tigers were female. And in olden times, people used to refer to tigers as "Grandmother Tiger." However, many of today's scholars who research the Dangun Myth consider the tiger male.

Even Kim Mu-jo, who agreed that the tigers as Sanshin were female, considered the specific tiger in the Dangun Myth male. According to Kim, the bear had been the tiger's wife, and the grief of losing his wife to Hwan-Ung became one of the founding themes in the development of Korean literature. In my opinion, the tendency of Korean scholars wanting to only interpret the tiger as male is due to their limited mindset or ignorance regarding gender culture and study.

The Dangun Myth explains that the tiger failed to become human due to the failure to endure the instructed seclusion away from the sunlight. Both bears and tigers usually live in caves, so the challenge, in this case, was avoiding sunlight. As the tiger also wished to become human, it went with the bear to pray to Hwan-Ung, ate the same herbs, and followed the directions of seclusion in the dark until it could do it no longer.

It is uncertain how long the tiger lasted following Hwan-Ung's instructions of 100 days of seclusion in the dark. Since the bear was successful in just 21 days, one can assume the tiger lasted between 1–20 days. Most scholars conclude that the tiger's failure is due to a lack of patience. On the other hand, patience in suffering and submission to authority (as the bear did) are culturally regarded as two of the most important virtues for Korean women.

Now let's review what the tiger failed at and why. What was the task that the tiger was unable to fulfill? What did the time away from the sunlight represent? The text of the myth only explains that the tiger was unable to follow through with the instructions; nothing else is described. In other foundation myths of ancient kingdoms of Korea, sunlight is frequently used to refer to the conception of the heir of Heaven. The founding myth of the Goguryeo Kingdom of Jumong is written in *Samguk Yusa*:

As Kumwa confined Yuwha, the daughter of Habaek,[20] in a dark room, the bright sunlight followed Yuwha's body and cast its rays on her body long and tenderly. Through this, Yuwha became pregnant, and finally birthed a giant egg.

"Seeing the sunlight" is certainly relevant to the motif of conception. As the story above demonstrates, the sunlight does not refer to broad daylight in an open space; it is the sunlight inside seclusion in the dark. In the story, the dark cave of the bear and the tiger is comparable to a dark room. Considering the background of these myths was an agricultural society, the symbolism of the sunlight as giving life to the grains can be equated to the sexual encounter between a man (the heavens) and a woman (the earth). If this is the case, we can interpret that avoiding sunlight in the myth signified female chastity or virginity.

The tiger clearly ate the herbs that are relevant to female sexuality, then the tiger had to stay in the dark cave without seeing other men. Therefore, it is possible to conclude that this means the tiger was unable to abstain from sexual relations. The tiger gave in to the temptation and failed. With her taboo broken and her isolation ended, her honor was lost.

The failure of the tiger represents how ancient Korean society viewed female sexuality. It defines female sexuality that is not linked to motherhood as a failure. This story shows how ancient Korean patriarchy tried to divide the female sex into two categories. Similarly, the ancient Greeks divided women into two categories:

---

20)   The god of River Aprok appears in different versions of Korean myths.

those of undisciplined threat to social order and those of controlled reproductive "*gyne*."

Whereas the bear represents motherhood, the tiger represents female sexuality. This paradoxical divide—that without female intercourse, conception leading to motherhood cannot exist—serves as a splitting of womankind in Korean society. By defining only the bear's case as a success, motherhood is endorsed as the only road to success for Korean women. The failed tiger represents the fear that some females—those who do not reproduce—may not enter the category of "women" (i.e., those capable of bearing children for society).

Considering that the bear and the tiger initially started in the same situation, one can argue that they both share the conditions of Korean women that must become "the Korean woman." The bear and the tiger are at opposite ends of that spectrum. The bear's female identity is expressed only at the cost of annihilating the other. Motherhood only comes after the denial of her sexuality. Thus, the tiger is the other half—the lost half—of herself.

Conclusion

Myth is always an account of a "creation." Stories of the supernatural explain how our reality came into existence. The reality of Korean women derived from the myth of Ung-Nyeo is not a pleasant one. As many social anthropologists are aware, myths play a role in explaining and justifying specific traditions and attitudes—for better or for worse.

As Eliade explained, "the myth is not an idle tale, but a hard-worked active force." By identifying this "hard-worked active force" in the story of Ung-Nyeo, I aim to identify Korean thoughts and attitudes about women. The Korean version of sexism, established and enshrined through the myth of Ung-Nyeo, can be summarized into three aspects.

First, the superiority of the male sex was justified by the three male generations' inherent divinity, while the bear-woman's origin is an earthly animal. All human relations are rooted in the union between man and woman. The implication of the heavenly man and the earthly woman relationship is that between god (divine being) and animal (lowly being), which led to the sexual dualism thriving in Korean society.

In a cosmic view, heaven (*yang*) dominates earth (*yin*), and correspondingly, males have precedence over females. This clear hierarchy is further described in the Confucian view that holds men in higher regard than women. This philosophy of male dominance has been one of the most influential beliefs throughout Korean history and has been the standard until recently.

Second, female submission to patriarchal traditions was solidified by positioning women under a hierarchy of three generations of men (father, husband, and son). Women do not have such traditions. Only the bloodlines of men are documented and dominant, leaving women to stand alone among three generations of men. Female submission to patriarchal traditions confined Korean women inside the house and made it possible for men to rule over every aspect of their lives.

Thus, women had no other choice but to be submissive to men. Before marriage, a woman was obedient to her father; when married, to her husband; and if her husband dies, then to her eldest son. This lifelong female subjugation later became articulated as the Confucian "three principles of life," those principles being that a woman must obey her father, husband, and son all her life.

Third, a polygamous tradition was justified by positioning one male (Hwan-Ung) and two females (Bear and Tiger) nonhierarchically. This polygamy was also applied to the heavens, as Hwan-Ung was a son of a concubine of Hwan-In. This means that polygamous practices were justified and permitted by the gods. This tradition led to subsequent divisions in women's relationships. Women were divided into two: those who could give birth to a son and those who couldn't.

Ung-Nyeo is simultaneously a cultural product of the archaic Korean mind and the manifestation of the ideological formation of "woman." Psychic impulses compel the creation of myths, but once inscribed and disseminated, myth reinforces, legitimates, and even influences the perpetuation of those impulses by authoritative powers. There is continuing reciprocity between the external and internal and between the individual psyche and collective ideology, which gives myth its dynamic life.

By unwrapping the clear "logic" portrayed in the myth, we can accept the presence of myth as a manifestation of the human consciousness and all the essential constituents of the myth. We can also reveal the manipulative function of the myth in society. Women's lost sexuality in the Korean Ung-Nyeo Myth is an intentional byproduct of this mythmaking.

The End

www.ingramcontent.com/pod-product-compliance
Lightning Source LLC
Chambersburg PA
CBHW031440200726
48289CB00007BB/1965